THE ART OF MURDER

A PARKER LEE MYSTERY

M.P. BLACK

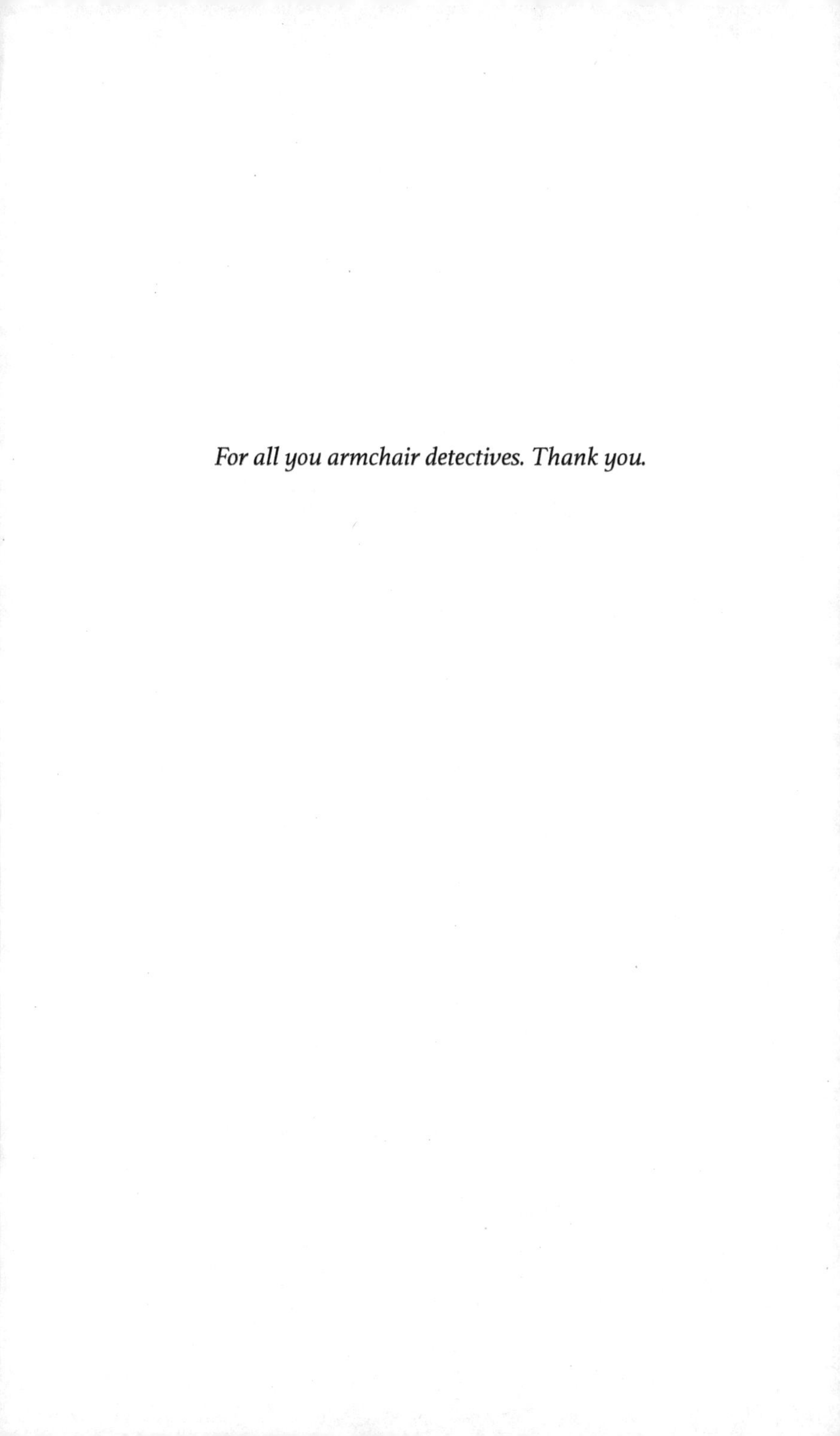

For all you armchair detectives. Thank you.

1

My quirky Aunt Lil and I were standing on the back porch of her boutique hotel. We both leaned on the railing—me drinking coffee, she drinking nettle tea. Both of us admiring the view of the lake. It's not called Lakeview Inn for nothing.

"Who's that?"

Mist shrouded the little island half a mile out—Gull Island—and caught a figure in a rowboat. Then the person hauled on the oars with determination and escaped the fog. The prow cut a rippling line across the smooth lake as the boat headed toward the town docks.

"Whoever it is, he's out early," Aunt Lil said. "Or she—I can't tell."

The mug warmed my cold hands, and I took another sip. The thin hoodie I wore couldn't keep out the cool, morning air. I shivered a little. Aunt Lil, who wore her usual billowy muumuu, along with her talisman necklaces and jangly bangles, didn't seem fazed by the cold.

I said, "I'll need to leave for the symposium soon."

"And I want to spend some time clearing out more junk in the attic before the guests wake."

"Lots of guests?"

"Full house. The symposium's a hit."

I gave myself another 5 minutes. I took a deep breath. The air, cooled by the night, was as fresh as spring water. What could be better than early mornings in Allington? In the city, at this hour, there would be no rowboat gliding through an ethereal mist, only cars and trucks rumbling through smog.

The hinges on the door behind us creaked, then smacked shut, as someone stepped out onto the porch.

"There you are, Parker. Morning, Lil."

Mom joined us, leaning against the railing. In her police uniform, she contrasted sharply with her sister. In most things, she contrasted with her sister.

Aunt Lil said, "How's law and order, Charlie?"

"So far, so good."

"Well, I'll leave you two Lees alone. My attic needs some order."

Aunt Lil headed inside through the door that connected the porch to the inn's lounge. Even after the door closed, I could hear the jangling of her bangles.

Mom's uniform was, as always, neatly pressed. On her chest, the badge that said "Chief" shone. So did the brass name tag with "C. Lee" engraved. Both spotless.

She looked out at the lake.

"Who's out there?"

"I was wondering about that," I said.

"Strange to be rowing back from the island this early."

"Maybe it's a fisherman."

In that instant, the rowboat vanished, slipping behind the town's main docks and out of sight.

I took another sip of coffee. The sun made an appearance. Across Allington Cove, on the opposite headland of our little cove, a big Victorian mansion, like the Lakeview Inn, glowed in the light. Broadstairs House. My childhood home. Which I'd returned to after leaving the city.

I'd dreamed of a successful career in journalism in the city, and it hadn't worked out. After coming back home, I'd felt ashamed. But I fallen in love with Allington all over again. It was where I belonged.

Although sometimes I still missed the action—the sensational stories—of the big city.

I forced my attention from the lake to my little town—and up Chestnut Hill to Larke House. The symposium would be starting soon. On the lake, the mist was growing thinner as the sun rose higher over the woods.

"Strange," Mom repeated, still staring toward the docks. "What was he doing out there?"

"Probably nothing news worthy," I said.

Mom glanced at me.

"You've got somewhere to be this morning. Otherwise you wouldn't sound so dismissive."

"Dad wants me to cover the symposium at Larke House."

"Of course. A couple of hundred art historians convening to discuss Julia Larke's life and legacy."

"You sound like the symposium program."

I dug up the rolled-up program out of the back pocket of my jeans and waved it at her to show I was already up to speed.

"Miranda gave me tons of reading material," I said. "She sure makes Larke sound important. But then that's her job, right—to make Julia Larke sound important?"

"Larke is important," Mom corrected me. "Here in Allington we've always known her artwork was special.

Imagine if she finally gets the worldwide recognition she deserves. That's a big deal." Then she smiled. "Besides, it's Joy's favorite artist."

My older sister Joy owned Cafe Larke, Allington's coziest coffee house. Larke's artwork decorated the walls of the cafe as well as Joy's bedroom at Broadstairs House. And she could recite an endless ream of facts about the artist's life. Even before Miranda, the director of Larke House, gave me a heap of reading material, I'd heard a lot about Julia Larke. But I'd never been especially interested.

I swirled the coffee in my cup. Almost empty. Almost time to go.

Mom said, "You're dragging your feet. Don't you want to do this assignment?"

"I thought Dad was doing it."

Mom said nothing. Forget about the gun she carried— silence was her most powerful weapon.

I sighed. "No, I don't want to do it. The news story about the symposium will be dry, boring stuff. Paint-by-numbers journalism."

"Not like the stories you covered in the big city."

"I didn't say that."

Mom said no more. She was staring at me with that familiar stony-faced look. The silent interrogation. Waiting for the person in the hot seat to break down and blab. I could pretend not to notice, but Chief of Police Lee could play this game until the sun set, and I had an assignment today.

"All right," I said with a sigh. "The stories aren't like the ones I covered in the big city."

"Every story in *The Gazette* can't be about fraud or murder."

"That's what Dad told me. 'A news article about a

murder can be ten times as boring as one about a lost kitten. It's all about how you tell the story.'"

"Your dad's a wise man," Mom said.

"And you're a little biased."

"Forty years of bias." She smiled. "But I can objectively say your dad knows what he's talking about."

She was right, of course. Dad ran *The Allington Gazette*, the local newspaper, carrying on a tradition that stretched back generations. If anyone knew about local news reporting, it was my dad.

I drained the dregs from my coffee cup. "Dad's right. It's all about how you tell the story. And that's why I'm going to get to Larke House early and give this story a decent shot. Like you said, it's a big deal that Julia Larke is finally getting the recognition she deserves."

I lifted my messenger bag off the deck and slung it over my shoulder.

Mom put a hand on my arm, stopping me.

"Park," she said. "I'm glad you're back."

"I'm glad I'm back, too."

"I just want you to know that I'm aware it hasn't been easy. I know Allington isn't as exciting as—"

Something crashed above us, and I jumped.

I looked up, and so did Mom.

A window flew open under the eaves of the roof.

"Charlie," Aunt Lil yelled. "I could use some of that law and order up here—and I'm not talking about organizing boxes."

2

Mom and I scrambled up the stairs to the inn's top floor. We hustled down a narrow corridor, which turned out to be the wrong one. Then almost passed the chamber—no bigger than a closet—where a ladder rose to the attic trapdoor.

"Even after Lil's renovations, this is still a maze," Mom said, gripping the rungs of the ladder. She began to scale the ladder and I followed. "You remember when it was the old Pullman?"

"Of course. The haunted house."

"You kids loved it. But it was a nightmare. Every year, some kid would fall through rotting floorboards or cut their hands on a broken window. I'm glad your aunt bought the place and fixed it up. She gave it a new life."

Mom vanished through the trapdoor opening and I followed her, hauling myself into the attic.

Long dusty floorboards extended to shadowy corners. Under the sloping ceiling stood boxes and old furniture. How anyone had ever managed to haul anything up here

was a mystery to me. Before they abandoned the house, the Pullmans must've had a different attic entrance. Where was it now? Hidden somewhere, no doubt. Pullman House used to have a reputation for boarded-up doors and secret passageways.

Aunt Lil stood near the trapdoor. She was holding a broomstick, apparently as a makeshift weapon. Her attention was on the other end of the attic. A man stood there. A piece of paneling lay at his feet, and an opening in the wall revealed a canvas in a simple wooden frame.

"That's Joe Rudder," she said. "A guest at the inn—I caught him trespassing."

"I was taking a look around—what's wrong with that?" he said.

He glanced at Mom in her uniform. Then ducked his head, as if he were trying to make himself smaller, less visible.

He looked about 50 years old, maybe older, with a ragged, gray-streaked beard. His brown houndstooth suit needed pressing. So did his face. Deep folds sagged under his eyes and broken capillaries blotched his skin.

"I caught Joe here rummaging in my attic," Lil explained. "And I thought, 'Hey, what could be so interesting about all this old junk?' Then I saw he was opening this panel in the wall. Lo and behold, there was a painting hidden inside."

She gestured at the painting.

"I found it," Joe snapped. "Finder's keepers. It's only fair..."

Mom said, "Lil is right. You're trespassing. This is her property—and so is that painting."

Joe raised his hands in a gesture of surrender. "Hey, I

meant no harm. I was only wandering the hallways, taking an interest in this beautiful old inn."

While they talked, I stepped up to the painting.

It showed a lake on a sunny day with a little tree-covered island off to the left. Up in the right-hand corner, a white blur moved against the blue sky—a bird. The resemblance to Lake Allington was striking.

The style was striking, too: quick, bold brushstrokes that gave each shape movement. Impressionist. I dug into my messenger bag for the Julia Larke Symposium program. Then compared the images within to the painting in front of me. I was no expert, but it looked a lot like Larke's artwork.

"You found this hidden in the wall?" I said.

Joe Rudder nodded.

"I'm not surprised," Aunt Lil said with a frown on her face. "He's a Scorpio, and right now, Scorpio, ruled by Pluto, craves the clandestine. But beware—" She brandished the broomstick at Joe Rudder. "—because Mars joins the lunar tides. Mars, the warrior. Mars, the bringer of destruction."

Joe Rudder touched his neck, looking uncomfortable.

Aunt Lil lowered the broomstick and added calmly, "Anyway, I'm also not surprised, because when I was renovating, I discovered something similar. It was in what used to be the master bedroom—a sliding panel in one of the closets. There was nothing inside the secret compartment. I'm guessing the owners, when they left, took whatever they'd been hiding. But they must've forgotten this one."

"It looks like a painting by Julia Larke," I said.

Joe let out a sound, as if to protest. Then stopped himself and instead glared at me.

I said, "Julia Larke spent time with French and American impressionists. But the establishment never recognized her. That's the whole point of the symposium—welcoming

Larke's artwork into the pantheon of American impressionists."

Mom glanced at me. "Establishment? Pantheon? You've been doing your homework."

"Guilty as charged. Miranda's indoctrinating me."

"Speaking of Miranda," Mom said to Aunt Lil. "You should take this painting to her. She'll know whether it's real or not, and how valuable it is."

Joe cut in. "Look, I helped you find it. It's only fair I get first dibs on buying it."

"What makes you think I'd sell?" Aunt Lil said. "I like it. A painting of the lake view is perfect for the Lakeview Inn." She cocked her head, studying the painting. Then nodded. "Yes, you know what? I'm going to keep it."

"That's crazy. Why hang on to this? At best, it's a lesser work—assuming it even is an original Larke."

He stared at Aunt Lil with an intense gaze. Something he'd said caught my attention. I said, "Wait a minute—you know about Larke and her artwork? Did you come here for the symposium?"

"The symposium," he said, and there was a dismissive tone to his voice. Then he seemed to realize something and changed tack. "Yeah, that's right. I'm here for the symposium."

"And wandering around the inn's attic," Mom said, "you just happened to stumble on a painting by Julia Larke?"

"Correct," he said. Defiant. But not so defiant that he dared look Mom in the eye.

Obviously, Mom didn't believe him. I didn't either. But what a strange thing to lie about. Why was he rummaging around in Aunt Lil's attic? And if he wasn't part of the symposium, how come he knew about Larke's artwork?

I was about to ask him more questions when my phone buzzed in my pocket.

It was Miranda.

Didn't we agree to meet now?

I let out a colorful curse that made Aunt Lil laugh and Mom frown, and I turned to the trapdoor.

"I'm late. Talk later."

3

At Larke House, a dozen symposium attendees clustered by the entrance, while others wandered through the wide open doors of the massive Victorian mansion. Miranda Gotschall stood on the front steps, picking at a button on her sleeve, looking impatient.

Her coat's design—a wild splatter of color—conveyed the energy of abstract expressionism. But Miranda's face looked pale, as if she hadn't been sleeping enough.

"You're late," she said.

"Sorry. I had to stop at the Lakeview. My aunt found a painting."

I filled her in on Aunt Lil's discovery, and Miranda raised an eyebrow.

"That would be something—discovering a missing Larke painting during the symposium."

"Exciting, right?" I said. "It could add some pizzazz to the story."

"Well, maybe. Larke painted dozens and dozens of views of Lake Allington, so even if it is an original, it wouldn't be worth much."

Someone nearby said, "You'd better leave that assessment to someone who knows."

Miranda grimaced as a woman approached.

"Hello, Esther."

"Miranda, you look—" the newcomer said, eyeing Miranda up and down, "—a little worse for wear. It must be a stretch for you to run something as big and professional as a symposium."

Miranda said, "Parker Lee, meet Esther Winch."

Esther Winch, in her late forties I guessed, wore a scarf that rivaled Miranda's coat in colorfulness. Her hair was a gray bird's nest. And she clutched a leather purse to her chest, as if she were afraid someone would snatch it.

"Another Larke enthusiast?" Esther asked.

"I'm a journalist with *The Allington Gazette*," I explained.

"Ah, the local rag." Esther looked around. "But where are the heavy hitters—the ones from *The New York Times* and *The Washington Post*? Oh, dear, Miranda. Couldn't manage to attract them to your little gathering?"

Miranda remained stoic in the face of these attacks. No placating smile. No defensive posture. As if Esther's nastiness was nothing new.

"How do you know each other?" I asked.

"Esther and I did our PhDs under the same professor," Miranda said. "Both of us specialized in American impressionism with a focus on Julia Larke. Esther chose to stay at the university, while I—"

"—while you grabbed the cookie jar and ran back home."

Esther was staring at Miranda. A fierce gaze. But Miranda only sighed.

"Nobody grabbed anything."

"If you hadn't published that book before mine was ready—"

"Your book was wonderful, and it did fine."

"You cannibalized my sales. Ate them right up. And the reviewers—they basically said one book on Larke was more than enough. But if my book had come first—"

"We should go inside," Miranda said to me, cutting off Esther. "The plenary session will begin soon."

"Which I'm sure will be a hoot," Esther said, breaking away.

Once she was out of earshot, I said, "You two don't get along..."

Miranda held up a hand. "Don't ask. I don't have the energy to discuss Esther Winch right now. Let's talk about Julia Larke instead, okay?"

"All right."

Miranda led me inside.

Larke House, Julia Larke's birth home, might be the biggest Victorian mansion on Chestnut Hill. And that was saying something, because there were lots of big Victorians on the Hill, the traditional home of Allington's upper class.

Julia's father owned the lumber business that fueled much of Allington's economy in the late 19th and early 20th centuries. Inside the mansion, the family's wealth was easy to see. Marble floors. Crystal chandeliers. A massive portrait of the patriarch and his wife and children—impossible to miss on the way through the entrance hall.

Signs with arrows guided symposium guests through the house. Miranda explained that almost 150 academics, program officers from art foundations, and even a few journalists had bought tickets to attend the three-day conference. It was the first of its kind to honor and explore the art and life of Julia Larke. But for the plenary session, which was open to the public, she expected as many as 300 people.

"Larke House is huge," she said, "but we can't accommodate so many people inside. So we've set up the symposium stage in the garden."

"Garden" sounded quaint. But Larke House's backyard was the size of a public park. Clusters of trees ringed a pond. A greenhouse stood near a fountain. At the far end of the garden stood a wrought-iron gate—a private entrance to Allington's cemetery. But it was the symposium setup that dominated the view: rows and rows of folding chairs and a small stage for the speakers.

Up above us, the sky was blue. An occasional cloud made a passing appearance, leaving the sun to blaze uninterrupted. But the air was fresh, not hot.

"Perfect weather for an outdoor event," I said.

"Lucky," Miranda said, and she grimaced. "So far."

Attendees already occupied most chairs, and one of Miranda's staff members ran up to her. They conferred about the seating. Would there be enough? What if they ran out of extra chairs? They both left, frowns on their faces, to deal with this crisis.

I managed to find an empty spot among the attendees. I opened my messenger bag and brought out a notepad and pen. As I waited for the show to begin, I jotted down a few notes.

Esther Winch - who is she?

Esther + Miranda: academic rivalry

Lil's Julia Larke painting: real? worth anything?

A man and a woman next to me argued about the enduring legacy of American impressionism. They used a lot of big words.

Then the man put a hand on the woman's arm and said, "Wait, is that—?"

The woman turned, looking in his direction. "You're right, it is."

"I didn't expect him to show up."

"Me neither."

They were looking at a tall man in his mid- to late 60s with wavy white hair and a tailored tweed suit. He exuded class and confidence.

I leaned toward my neighbors and said, "Sorry, who is he?"

"Knox Kensington, of course," the woman said, looking down her nose at me.

"And he is...?"

"Head of the Fine Art Department at Bishop & Company—you know, the famous auction house."

I nodded. I'd heard of it.

The man said, "You think Knox is here to snatch up another Larke painting?"

"Why else? After his recent success...well, he may not think much of Larke, but if an artist smells of money, he'll come sniffing, won't he?"

They both laughed. The image of the distinguished Knox Kensington as a dog must be amusing. But as Knox passed their row, the man shot to his feet and stuck out his hand.

"Mr. Kensington," he said. "Such an honor to meet you. Such an honor. Harold Foster from Kemp College. Head of the Fine Arts Department. You'll no doubt know my work on the *plein air* movement and Benson, in particular. My articles are published in—"

"I'm afraid I don't," Knox cut the man off. He disengaged from the handshake. "Now, excuse me."

"Of course, of course—the show's about to begin. Such a pleasure to talk to you. Such a pleasure."

Harold Foster gazed after the tall man leaving, a fawning smile on his face.

But when he turned back to his companion, he dropped the servile attitude and said, "What a snob."

The woman agreed, and soon they'd returned to their conversation about impressionism.

Obviously, there was a hierarchy to the art world—and Knox Kensington must be one of the top dogs.

A moment later, Miranda took to the stage. The attendees applauded. She tapped the microphone and said, "Welcome, everyone."

She spoke about the purpose of the event and how Julia Larke was rising from obscurity to become recognized as an important link in the chain of American impressionists. She compared Larke with John Leslie Breck, Childe Hassam, and Mary Cassatt.

I was jotting down notes, careful not to miss out on anything.

Then something stung my neck.

I dropped my pen and put my hand to my skin, rubbing it.

A bug?

If so, it didn't have much of a sting.

Then it happened again: a sharp prick, and I flinched.

Not a sting. Something had struck my neck. I looked around and saw only academics in the row behind me, all of them staring at the stage. On the grass, two pieces of paper, folded into triangles, lay between a man's feet. I couldn't reach them where they'd fallen, so I turned back around.

The third time it happened, the object hit my shoulder instead and tumbled onto my lap.

"What the...?"

It was a another piece of paper, folded into a hard triangle. That was what had "stung" me.

I unfolded the one in my hands. Inside was a note:

Jeez, Park. Pay attention to the teacher, will you?

Something stirred in me—an old memory—and it made me smile. I turned in my seat and scanned the crowd. Bingo. There he was: two rows behind me, grinning at me like a lunatic.

"Teddy Kendall," I muttered, smiling. "What the heck are you doing here?"

4

"Park," Teddy said when I caught up with him after Miranda's opening speech. "Funny bumping into you."

"You're back in Allington," I said.

"Only for this event. And you? Are you visiting?"

"No," I said, feeling awkward, "I'm living here now."

But he didn't ask what happened to my career in the city —or why I'd ever think of moving back home. Instead, he smiled and nodded and said, "Allington's such an amazing town. It must feel nice to come home. Are you at the symposium for work—or just out of curiosity?"

I smiled. "Working."

I told him about my job at *The Gazette*.

"When I was a kid," he said, "my big dream was to become a reporter at *The Gazette*."

I nodded. "Your articles for the school paper were always so great. I remember you telling me you'd be a writer some day. Like Hemingway. Is that what you're doing now?"

He laughed. "You remember. That was indeed my inauspicious start to an illustrious career in writing. Although I'm nothing like Hemingway."

He explained that he'd built a career as a freelance writer, specializing in the art scene. When he heard about the Julia Larke symposium, he immediately saw an opportunity to visit his "old stomping grounds" while also making some money covering the event.

"Allington still feels like home," he said. "Like I belong here—and vice versa, like this town belongs to me. You know what I mean?"

"I know exactly what you mean."

We found a coffee station. We drank coffee from paper cups and talked about our childhood memories. Endless summers. Exploring the woods. Rowing out to Gull Island and exploring the old cabin ruin among the trees.

"Gull Island," Teddy said. "Can't say I've ever seen a gull out there."

"My dad says it's called Gull Island because of a Chekhov play that was performed there long ago."

"We used to call it Snake Island, remember?" he said.

"Which is funny," I said, "because I don't think I've ever seen a snake out there either."

"I did—or I thought I did—and it totally freaked me out. I hate snakes."

"Really? I remember you being fearless. Didn't you spend the night at the old Pullman House on a dare?"

Teddy nodded. "That was great. So creepy. But also so much to explore..." He sighed. "We had fun, didn't we?" A dark cloud passed over his face. "But that's a long time ago..."

Our conversation stalled. There was a piece of history he wasn't mentioning—when his parents sent him off to boarding school—but I didn't need him to bring it up. His face, sunk into gloom, hinted at his unhappiness after leaving Allington.

Did he want to talk about it? The silence extended. I let it grow.

Then I said, "So now you're a Julia Larke expert..."

Teddy brightened. "Hardly an expert, but I've done some research, and it's cool that she's finally getting the recognition she deserves. I mean, as a kid, her paintings seemed so spectacular, and everyone in town agreed what a talent she was. But how many small towns worship local heroes? To the outside world, they don't mean anything."

"Well, in Julia Larke's case, it seems the world is paying attention."

The squeak of the microphone interrupted our conversation. It was time to return to our seats for the next speech. The program said so-and-so would lecture on Larke's apprenticeship at the Giverny art colony in France.

As we headed back to our seats, Teddy pointed toward Knox Kensington. He stood nearby talking to Esther Winch.

"The famous Knox Kensington has graced us with his presence."

"So you know him?"

"Oh, I know them all. The Kensingtons, the Winches. You have to, if you want to write about this world." He glanced at me. "I'm not bragging, you know."

"I believe you. Actually, I was thinking..."

An idea had occurred to me. Teddy's knowledge of the art world could help me write about Julia Larke and the symposium. I linked arms with him and said, "Mind if I find a seat next to you? I want to pick your brain."

Teddy laughed. "Pick away."

5

"If you're such an expert, Teddy," I said with a wink, "tell us: real Julia Larke or fake?"

He cocked his head, studying Aunt Lil's new painting.

She'd hung it over the mantelpiece in the Lakeview Inn's lounge—where it was impossible to miss. Aunt Lil and I had been admiring it when Teddy joined us, drink in hand.

All around us—and outside on the back porch—people chatted and drank wine. Since talking to Teddy, I could identify many of them. My notebook was full of their names and connections to Julia Larke. I looked around to see who stood talking together.

The blinds were down in the lounge, shading us from the setting sun. But the door to the back porch stood open, and I glanced out. Joe Rudder passed by. He held a glass of wine in one hand and a canapé in the other. He shoved the food into his mouth and walked out of sight.

Where had he been today? Not at the symposium.

Knox Kensington passed by the door, too, a frown on his

face as he moved in the same direction. It almost looked as if he was following Joe—but maybe that was my imagination.

"You're taking your time," Aunt Lil told Teddy. "Are you a Virgo, by any chance?"

"I'm no expert," Teddy said, ignoring my aunt's question about his star sign. "But I'd say it's a fake. No offense."

I said, "What makes you say it's a fake? Something about the brush strokes?"

"No, no. Statistics. Most of these attic discoveries turn out to be nothing. But honestly, you'd need an expert to assess the painting. Hey, Miranda—"

Miranda, a glass of seltzer in hand, excused herself from a conversation and joined us. Teddy explained his theory about how improbable it was that this was an original Julia Larke.

"He's right," Miranda said. "Those multi-million-dollar discoveries you see on TV are rare. But this one..."

"You think it might be by Larke?" I asked.

"I can't say. Though calling it a 'fake' might be unfair. Julia Larke taught many locals to paint. She often used her own works as models for her students to copy, so there are many, many reproductions out there. Some good, some bad. This one could be a good copy. I'll have to take it off the wall and study it. When I have time."

"Even if it's not a real Julia Larke," Aunt Lil said, "I adore it, and it's hanging in the perfect spot, don't you think?"

"It is pretty," I agreed. "Is it safe, though? I mean, if it turns out to be a real Julia Larke, shouldn't we lock it up somewhere?"

"Lock it up?" Miranda said, giving me a disapproving frown. "Paintings shouldn't be locked up or hidden away."

"Don't worry," Aunt Lil said. "I placed crystals on the mantelpiece to ward off any negative energy."

I caught Miranda and Teddy exchanging incredulous glances.

But then Aunt Lil added, "Plus, I put a little alarm on the painting itself, which goes off if you try to move it."

I smiled. People often thought my aunt was a kook. But she hadn't made the Lakeview Inn a success simply by studying planetary alignments.

She said, "Anyway, look around. There are too many people around for a thief to walk off with my painting."

Miranda looked around. Her gaze settled on the door to the back porch. Knox Kensington peeked into the lounge, scanned the room, and then moved back out.

When Miranda turned back, she sighed.

"What is it?" I asked. "What's the big deal with Knox Kensington?"

"Oh, he's the head of the fine arts department at Bishop & Company—"

"I got all that. But what's he got to do with Julia Larke?"

"You haven't heard?" She frowned. "It's in the information packet I gave you."

I nodded. Like I'd had time to read the dozens of books and articles she'd shared ahead of the symposium. At least I'd read Miranda's own book on Larke.

She gave me a schoolmarmish look. Deep disapproval. Then explained. "Julia Larke painted a triptych—three canvases that belonged together—of three sisters. Nudes. People considered them risqué in her time, which may be why they disappeared."

"Now I remember—you call them 'The Lost Sisters' in your book," I said, nodding. "But other impressionists painted nudes, didn't they?"

"They did. And that was fine in Paris and New York, but the paintings ruffled feathers in provincial Allington. The lumber magnate's eccentric, independent daughter could paint landscapes. But painting three wealthy women in the nude? That shocked her contemporaries. So the three paintings were tucked away to avoid scandal. Which, if you ask me, was the real scandal. Because the three sisters triptych is undoubtedly Larke's masterpiece."

"I don't think I saw pictures of the three sisters in the book you lent me."

"You wouldn't have. Unlike her other pieces, they weren't copied or reproduced. And my book on Larke came out before the recent discovery."

"They found them?"

Miranda nodded. "A family in Boston found two of the three panels, concealed under canvases by one of Larke's students. And guess who's auctioning off the two sisters..."

"Bishop & Company?"

"That's right. Knox Kensington is in charge of the auction, and so I guess that's why he's taking an interest in Larke. Although he's dismissive of her impact on American impressionism as a whole. He calls her 'a poor man's Mary Cassatt.' And don't get him started on Mary Cassatt."

"But Cassatt is a famous artist," I said.

"She was also a woman," Miranda said. "And therefore, if you ask Knox, overrated."

"This Knox guy sounds charming," Aunt Lil said. "I can just imagine his aura will look like." She gave a little shudder.

"Are you bidding on the two sisters?" I asked Miranda.

Miranda shook her head. "I wish I could, but they're beyond what Larke House can afford. Ironic, isn't it? I've been working so hard to improve Larke's reputation. But now that it's finally happening, Larke House can't buy her most important paintings. Our endowment is too small. Our collection will remain strong, yet limited to the works that Larke kept in the family." She gazed up at the painting on the wall, a frown creasing her eyebrows. "I worry some wealthy private collector will buy the two sisters. Then hide them away in a vault somewhere, never to see the light of day again."

Her shoulders slumped. She ran a hand across her eyes, as if the light bothered her.

I flipped open my notepad and jotted down some of the details.

> *Three Sisters*
> Two found in Boston, auction by Bishop & Company
> Knox Kensington, dismissive of Larke (and other women)

One of Aunt Lil's servers passed us with a tray of drinks, and turned to offer us some white wine. I recognized her—a local teenager earning cash for her own college fund.

"No, thanks, Hannah," I said, smiling.

Esther Winch and Knox Kensington approached us. They grabbed each their glass without acknowledging Hannah. She might as well have been invisible to them.

Esther squinted at the painting on the wall.

"That's a copy," she said. "I'd bet money on it."

"And even if it's not," Knox said, "it's not exactly the pinnacle of impressionism, is it?" He gestured at a nearby antique table on which stood a marble bust of Marie Antoinette. "I bet this bust is 10 times the price. The marble itself must be worth a lot more than that painting."

Teddy jumped in. "Larke's reputation is increasing, Mr.

Kensington. Her paintings may not meet your high standards. But the consensus is changing—her genius is undeniable. And this painting is no exception."

"You can write that," Knox said. "You can even publish it. But you won't convince me."

"Your view on things is outdated," Teddy snapped, clenching his fists.

Knox snorted, turned, and wandered off. He took his time, passing an antique table and running a finger along it, as if to trace a line in dust that wasn't there.

Esther followed him, hurrying with short, anxious steps.

Miranda watched them with a frown on her face, then excused herself. "I've got to get ready for my speech out on the porch," she said.

Aunt Lil headed off to tend to her guests.

With the others gone, leaving only Teddy and me, I nudged my old school friend and smiled at him.

"You got pretty excited," I said.

Teddy ran a hand through his hair. "Yeah, I lost my cool."

"No, it was great. At first I thought you were dismissive of the painting. Then you came to Larke's defense. Heck, you came to Miranda's and even Allington's defense, too."

Teddy shrugged, staring up at the painting. "Sometimes it feels like you can't separate Larke from Allington. I guess it makes me defensive, especially around elitists like Knox Kensington."

"Good job telling him the truth," I said.

"The truth? I don't know about that. The truth is that Esther's right. It's most likely a copy. You heard Miranda. Larke's students made heaps and heaps of reproductions. Plus, she herself painted the same subject again and again.

She made slight variations or experimented with different colors."

"Like Monet's Water Lilies?" I asked.

"Exactly. Did you know Monet did more than 250 of them? If you study them all, it's fascinating to see his technique evolve. But it's for academics and obsessives. If the paintings weren't done by Monet, you'd look at three or four water lilies and then get bored."

"Wait," I said. "First you said the painting was a fake. Then you defended it as a genius, and now—now you agree with Esther and Knox?"

"I don't like those two snobs..." He shrugged. "But yeah, I agree with them."

6

"By joining me today, you are making history," Miranda said from the dock below us. We were all standing on the porch, crowding at the railing so we could see Miranda. "We are here because we recognize the growing importance of Julia Larke, one of America's foremost—and most neglected—female impressionists."

"Foremost?" Knox said nearby, his voice dripping with disdain, and a few people around him tittered.

Next to me, Esther frowned, a sour expression on her face. Miffed at her buddy Knox? I would be if I'd spent my career studying and promoting Julia Larke's art and then had to listen to his snooty comments.

"Look at that view," Aunt Lil said, distracting me from Esther and Knox. "It's like a nighttime version of my painting."

She was right. Dusk's deep, dark blue sky was darkening even more, and the moon shone with an uncanny brilliance. Its white light cast silver on the lake.

It reminded me of a painting at Larke House. It was

called "Moon over Allington." Could Aunt Lil's painting be a daytime variation of that other artwork?

A breeze swept over the lake. The chill tickled my neck and the door to the lounge shuddered in its frame. I wrapped my arms around myself.

A whisper followed the chill, like a breeze shushing in the leaves.

Or muffled voices muttering from the beyond.

That was the kind of thing Dad used to say when I was a kid: "muffled voices muttering from the beyond." He used to tell me long, rambling ghost stories that would build to an unbearable suspense. Delightful stuff. They'd always take place in Allington, too, which made them even more thrilling. Like the story of the banshee that used to haunt Pullman House. If Mom was around, she'd interrupt and fact check the story: "Fred, sweetie, that never happened. The Pullmans never saw a banshee in their attic. And whoever said anything about them having Scottish ancestry? That's a German name. More importantly, there's no such thing as ghosts."

"Almost a full moon," Aunt Lil said, her voice quiet, "its emotional amplification and, ultimately, culmination and release should put us all on guard."

"On our guard?" I whispered, goosebumps forming on my arms. "On our guard against what?"

Aunt Lil shrugged. "Oh, you know: cosmic forces, the shadow realm, the—"

An ear-piercing, rapid-fire beeping shattered the mood, drowning out Miranda's voice. Heads turned. The noise was coming from inside. From beyond the lounge door.

Bee—bee—bee—bee—bee—

"The alarm," Aunt Lil said.

"Quick," I said.

I turned and bolted toward the lounge door. A man with a glass of wine in each hand floundered in my path, yelling, "Doris, Doris, where did you go?"

People turned to look and ask questions. Some pushed in one direction, while others wanted to go the opposite way. Blocking my way.

"Emergency," I yelled. "Move, please!"

But no one listened.

Then Aunt Lil appeared behind me and, raising her arms so her bangles slid down with a series of clinks, keened like a banshee.

It was as if she'd fired a cannon ball through the crowd—people leaped aside, startled, and the sea of bodies parted.

"Go ahead, Park," she said, nudging me forward.

I tore open the door to the lounge. The alarm grew louder.

Bee—bee—bee—bee—bee—

I slipped inside and Aunt Lil followed close behind.

Across the lounge, the other door slammed shut.

"Who was that?"

"Don't know," Aunt Lil yelled over the ear-deafening alarm.

The spot over the mantlepiece—where the painting had hung—was empty.

"The painting!"

I hurried forward, passing the antique table on my way to the door. Glancing toward the hearth, I saw something. What was that on the floor?

I froze.

A man. He lay spread out on the oriental rug, flat on his stomach. Sticking out underneath him was the painting.

The back of his head was a bloody mess.

Bee—bee—bee—bee—bee—

Aunt Lil and I approached the man, crouching down by his side. Aunt Lil reached under the painting and fumbled with the alarm.

Bee—bee—bee—

The beeping stopped. The sudden silence hit me like a ton of bricks.

I stared at the man. At the bloody mess. The silence seemed to deepen.

I took a deep breath and focused. I'd seen worse working as a reporter in the city. Stabbings. Death by overdose. Bodies dragged out of the water, unrecognizable.

This at least was straightforward. I knew him. He wore the same rumpled houndstooth suit he'd worn that morning.

"It's Joe Rudder," I said.

"Is he drunk?" a voice said behind me.

I jumped and looked over my shoulder.

Esther. Where the heck did she come from?

But she wasn't the only one who'd come into the lounge. People streamed inside, no doubt curious about the alarm. A man with a ridiculous handlebar mustache said, "Jeez, is this a joke or something?" Seeing the body, a woman staggered back and bumped into a Tiffany lamp. She said, "I didn't mean to—I'm sorry..."

Knox Kensington said, "Did someone call an ambulance?"

"I'm on it," Aunt Lil said, phone pressed to her ear.

Teddy crouched down by Joe and put two fingers against his neck. After a while, he met my gaze.

"No pulse," he said. "He's dead."

7

Deputy Douglas stuck his head through the door to the lounge. "Chief Lee, all done. Everyone's either outside or in their rooms."

"Everyone but Teddy here," Mom said.

"I'd like to stay," Teddy said. "I'm covering the Larke symposium and—"

"I know why you're back in Allington. But this is a crime scene."

Teddy shoved his hands in his pockets and jerked his head at me and Dad. "But they get to stay?"

I cringed. What gave *The Allington Gazette* special privileges at a crime scene? It didn't have anything to do with me being the chief of police's baby daughter, now did it? Or with the owner of *The Gazette* being my dad?

Mom said, "Fred stays. And Parker and Lil, too. I'd like to talk to them about what happened. After all, they found the body."

"I was here too."

"Don't worry—we'll want to talk to you as well." Mom nodded at Deputy Douglas. "Deputy."

Deputy Douglas put a hand on Teddy's arm, but Teddy shrugged him off. "Don't touch me."

He strode out of the lounge, slamming the door behind him. Deputy Douglas pulled it open again and followed Teddy outside.

"Hmm…" Aunt Lil said. "I very much doubt he's a Virgo. More likely an Aries."

"Let's get back to work," Mom said, plowing on as if nothing had disturbed her equilibrium. "We've got a dead man, apparently the victim of severe head trauma inflicted by persons unknown."

Dad crouched down by a table near the back wall. He looked up and said, "My money's on Marie Antoinette. She did it."

He pointed. Under the table lay the marble Marie Antoinette bust. The one Knox Kensington had compared with the Julia Larke painting. It seemed to have rolled under the table, coming to rest on its side.

Marie Antoinette gazed up at us. She looked bored. Despite the smear of blood on her forehead.

Dad straightened up with a grunt, grasping his knees to push and steady himself. He was going on 70 years old, big-bellied and jovial. A contrast to Mom's lean, straight-backed figure. His flushed face reminded me how much he liked good food and wine. He wore a knit fisherman sweater—he always did, even in the worst of heat waves—and it suited his white beard.

"So, the killer clobbers Joe Rudder on the head," he said. "Joe collapses onto the Larke painting. The killer dashes out."

Mom said, "None of which tells us who did it or why." She turned to Aunt Lil. "What did you notice when you came into the lounge?"

"The alarm, of course. My mind was on the painting, and then I saw it was missing from over the mantlepiece."

"The door," I added. "Someone slammed the door."

Aunt Lil nodded. "That's right. The door to the hallway. A shadowy someone shut it. Before I could cross the room and see who was running away, I saw Joe lying on the floor—actually on top of my painting—and I forgot all about whoever slammed the door."

"Deputy Douglas searched the inn," Mom said. "As I'd expected, he found nothing suspicious. The hallway leads to the reception—and the stairs going up."

"And the other direction to the dining room," Aunt Lil said.

"Any exits from the dining room?"

"There are doors to the kitchen and the porch."

"Ah."

"'Ah,' what?" I asked.

"Well, if we assume it was the killer who slammed the door, then he or she could've slipped through the dining room and back out onto the porch to join the crowd."

Aunt Lil said, "Or they could've gone through the reception, out the front door, and followed the porch around to the back. It wraps all the way around."

"Good point. Either way, the killer could've rejoined the party. The question is whether anyone noticed. We'll talk to everyone involved, of course. But something tells me your alarm provided a helpful distraction."

"Distraction or no distraction," Dad said, "the killer was pretty daring."

"So was Joe Rudder," Mom said. "If we assume he was the one trying to steal the painting, then he did it while the entire symposium was gathered outside the door to the porch. Why? Why not sneak in here during the symposium when everyone was at Larke House?"

"Because not everyone was at Larke House," Aunt Lil said. "I was preparing for tonight's reception. The extra staff I hired were in and out of this room constantly, and so was I. Plus, someone was always on the back porch or in the reception. Joe simply wouldn't have had the chance to steal the painting and get it out."

While my aunt talked, I crouched down by Joe's body again. How strange that only hours ago, I'd been talking to him. Now he was dead.

Fact number one: he was dead. What else could I learn from him?

His wrinkled suit suggested he wasn't rich. But he wasn't wearing old jeans and a ragged t-shirt, either. Maybe it meant Joe Rudder wanted to appear classy, even if he wasn't. He aspired to greater things.

I noticed something else nearby: a dark shadow on the rug.

I inched closer. It wasn't a shadow. It was a footprint.

"Look at this," I said.

"What've you found?" Mom said, coming to my side.

"A footprint. Looks like soot."

"Don't touch it. Forensics are on their way."

What, like I didn't know? I gave Mom a look, but her attention was on the footprint.

She said, "Maybe Joe stepped in the fireplace when he was grabbing the painting."

I studied the fireplace. The foundation required a single step up. The hearth stood wide open. No grate to keep someone from treading in the ashes.

I could picture it: Joe stepping up to the painting, grabbing it, and then turning to make a run for it.

I shifted around so I could look at his footwear. He wore canvas shoes with white rubber soles. The soles, though worn, weren't dirty. No soot.

So, he didn't step in the fireplace. The killer did.

A door opened. It was the door to lounge, the one from the reception, and several people filed inside. The bustle of professionals with cameras and forensic kits transformed the room. The county coroner greeted Mom and shot me a stern look. I backed off from the body.

The forensics team got busy taking photos and preparing to bag the evidence, including the painting. Mom shepherded us out the other door to the porch, leaving the crime scene to the coroner and his team. As I stepped out of the lounge, I glanced back at the scene of the crime and let out a sigh. What I wouldn't give to cover this story. It was a heck of a lot more interesting than the symposium, the latest bake sales at schools, or municipal plans to repave Main Street.

Outside on the back porch, the crowd of symposium guests had thinned, only a few stragglers remaining to gossip.I closed the door to the lounge behind me, intending to head over to Aunt Lil, who was leaning against the railing. But Mom blocked my way. Dad leaned against the wall next to me.

What was going on? Were they ganging up on me?

"Uh, I should get back to work," I said.

"I want you to cover this story," Mom said.

My heart did a little backflip. "Really?"

I glanced at Dad. He nodded.

Mom said, "You know how quickly people can clam up when the police come calling. You may discover something I won't."

"But Dad's a better journalist," I said. "More experienced."

"Which is a euphemism for old and slow," Dad said with a smile. He tapped his forehead. "If you need my wise, old brain, you know where to find it. But don't think you can get out of the other stories. A big city reporter like you should be able to juggle everything."

I smiled. "You got it."

By the time I reached Aunt Lil, I was full-out grinning.

8

Aunt Lil unlocked the door to Joe Rudder's room and Deputy Douglas pushed it open. He looked around, biting his lip. "Don't touch anything, okay?"

I stepped into the room and Aunt Lil followed me. It was a single room. The windows overlooked the street out front. Not the coveted lake view.

The bed dominated and left little room to maneuver around it. Two suitcases lay on the edge of the bedspread, both lids closed but with the clasps open, as if Joe had been packing. If so, he hadn't finished. In a corner behind the bed, he'd stacked something against a wall. A towel draped over the rectangular objects.

I moved around the bed and crouched down. Grabbing a pen from my messenger bag, I used it to lift the edge of the towel and peek underneath.

"Paintings."

"Careful," Deputy Douglas said from the other side of the bed, his voice a nervous squeak. "Chief Lee won't like it if we mess up evidence."

Aunt Lil looked over my shoulder as I added a second pen, using them like chopsticks to move one canvas and look at the next.

Both depicted natural landscapes in a generic 19th century painterly style. A waterfall cascading down rocks. A deer in a glade, caught in a ray of sunlight through the canopy. I'd seen paintings like these in motel rooms.

"I'm no expert, but these don't look like they'd be worth a lot."

Aunt Lil said, "I agree. I bet you could buy them for 10 or 15 bucks at a yard sale."

I flipped to the next canvas.

"And what about this one?"

Aunt Lil drew a sharp breath. "That's my painting."

"Then so is this one."

The two canvasses contained versions of the lake view that Joe Rudder had tried to steal. All three seemed to belong together—Aunt Lil's and these two. The color choices differed slightly, and there were other small varia-tions. No bird in the corner. But the upward strokes, the green leaves on the trees and the blue water rippling in the same way—they were the same.

"Did Julia Larke do these?" Aunt Lil asked. "They look like copies."

"I'm guessing they're variations."

"Practice makes perfect? Or one of Larke's students copying her work?"

"Miranda will know."

I brought out my phone and asked Aunt Lil to hold the canvases apart while I snapped pictures of the two lake paintings. Aunt Lil's grip on the pens slipped and she cursed as the canvasses toppled over.

"Careful!" Deputy Douglas said, his voice high-pitched.

He stepped toward us and knocked into one of the suit-cases on the bed. It slid off the edge and crashed to the floor, its contents spilling out.

He stood back and put a hand to his forehead.

"Oh, no," he groaned. "Oh, no..."

I got to my feet. The paintings could wait. A wealth of evidence lay spread out for us on the carpeted floor.

"Well done, Doug."

"What will Chief Lee say?"

"Don't worry about my mom. I'll take the blame. But look at this..."

The sheer variety of items on the floor amazed me. An antique model train. A stack of yellowed baseball cards held by a frayed rubber band. A handmade duck decoy. Several vintage Christmas ornaments.

Among the bric-a-brac lay a paperback memoir by Arthur X, the billionaire. Apparently, he loved art as much as himself. On the cover, he stood in front of his private heli-copter holding an antique Chinese vase. The title was *This Art Belongs to Art*.

But there was also this: flyers from garage sales, estate sales, and local auctions. Plus a thick antique pricing guide and an auction catalog—with a Julia Larke painting on the cover.

"Check out the title of the auction house on this cata-log," I said.

"Bishop & Company," Aunt Lil said.

"This must've been Joe's gig. He'd go looking for cheap antiques he could sell at a premium."

"Or original art he could sell for millions. It reminds me of a crazy story I read about..."

She told the story of a retired truck driver who found a painting in a thrift shop and bought it for 5 dollars. "Turned out, it was an original Jackson Pollack and worth about $140 million. Though my lake view, even if it is by Larke, won't be worth that much."

I said, "Let's check the catalog."

Deputy Douglas said, "No, no, let me."

He wore latex gloves. He turned over the auction catalog and opened it, flipping the pages with such care you'd think it was ancient parchment.

"Wait a second," I said.

He stopped flipping and I pointed at a spread that featured only two paintings. Both of nude women sitting in arm chairs.

"There they are," I said. "The two sisters that Knox Kensington is selling."

Aunt Lil leaned closer and let out a whistle. "Half a million each? Who can afford to pay that for a painting?"

"Not Larke House, according to Miranda."

Deputy Douglas continued to turn the pages. He came to one that was dogeared.

"There's your painting, Aunt Lil," I said. "Or something like it."

The catalog listed a dozen lake view paintings by Larke. They ranged from a $200 to $3,000.

Aunt Lil said, "Three grand is a nice chunk of change."

I looked around. The objects that had fallen out of Joe Rudder's suitcase ranged from pure junk to antique. They might be worth something, but not millions of dollars, not even thousands.

I said, "Joe Rudder was small-time. Let's say he thought your painting was a real Larke. He'd know he could sell it for a few hundred dollars—maybe even a couple of thousand. That would be worth stealing, wouldn't it?"

"Sure," Aunt Lil said.

"But who would want to stop him?"

"Someone who didn't want Larke's painting to end up on the black market?"

"Maybe. But why wouldn't that person raise the alarm and call the cops? Joe was seconds away from being caught in the act. Why kill him?"

Aunt Lil shook her head, no answer to the question.

Deputy Douglas didn't provide a theory. He was too busy staring at the objects lying on the floor, his face pinched. He rubbed his neck.

"What a mess," he muttered. "What a mess..."

9

The next morning brought bright sunshine. I scanned the line at the coffee station in Larke House's garden. Tired faces squinting at the sky. Everyone looked desperate for caffeine. The symposium guests must've stayed up late last night. No doubt gossiping about the murder. Or else frightened, going to sleep early, but waking every time the bed creaked.

Not Knox Kensington. He looked as stern and commanding as ever.

"Enjoying the symposium?" I said as I reached for a paper cup.

"Enjoyment has nothing to do with it," he said.

"But you must find it interesting."

"I find it—" He filled a cup with coffee and added milk and sugar. "—unavoidable."

He turned to leave. I maneuvered around him, blocking his way.

"Terrible thing about Joe Rudder."

"Yes."

"You knew him, of course."

Knox frowned. "Why would I know a low-life like that? I don't consort with art scavengers."

"Oh, of course you don't. And why would you, Knox Kensington, know someone like that?" I sipped my coffee and then added, "But then how did you know he was an art scavenger?"

He towered over me, glaring. Here was a man who could do a lot with his eyebrows to intimidate.

"Eyebrows don't frighten me," I told him, smiling.

His eyebrows faltered. A look of confusion flashed across his face. "Oh, never mind." He huffed, regaining his composure. "Excuse me." He snapped a lid on his cup, and strode away.

It was amazing how gratifying it could be to rattle an arrogant man. More important, though, he'd confirmed my suspicion: there was a link between him and Joe Rudder. But what was that link?

"He's a liar," a voice said beside me.

Esther Winch was standing there, a cup of milky tea in her hands, the string from the tea bag dangling over the rim.

"Oh?" I said. "And I thought you were friends."

"Don't be ridiculous. Knox doesn't have friends. You're either his ally or his enemy—or else you're simply part of the scenery."

"And which are you?"

Esther sipped her tea. "I'm pragmatic. But I wasn't talking about me. I was talking about Knox." She leaned closer to me, confiding. "Consider this: Knox claims Larke's art is subpar. But then why show up to the symposium?"

"Has he told you why?"

"Oh, he has some story about Bishop & Company handling Larke's art and his responsibility to the business. Blah, blah, blah."

"He told me he was here because it was 'unavoidable.'"

Esther snorted. "Typical Knox."

"You doubt his story?"

"Only a fool would believe that man," she said. "I hear the president of Bishop & Company wakes up in a cold sweat every night worrying about what Knox thinks of him. Knox gets a free rein at that auction house. You think he bothers with conferences he thinks are a waste of time?"

"But Larke's reputation is on the rise. He may not care about her art, but what about the value of the paintings?"

"He can sell paintings without going to academic conferences. Besides, I heard what you said about Joe Rudder. And Knox was lying. I overhead him talking to Rudder at the inn."

"How did they know each other?"

She shrugged. "No idea. But they must have. Why else should they have a heated conversation? I heard them on the back porch. It was quite a confrontation."

"What did they say?"

She waved a hand. "Oh, I couldn't hear. But it's like I said: either Rudder was Knox's ally or enemy. If he was neither, Knox wouldn't give him the time of day." She gripped my arm hard. "This is all hearsay, of course. You can't print hearsay in that little newspaper of yours. Or can you?" Her face cracked into a broad grin, revealing tea-stained teeth. "I bet you can. I can see it now: an exposé of Knox Kensington. A takedown. What do you say?"

Esther clung to me, and I tried to break free. Not only because her suggestion was offensive. Her breath reeked of something strong. That tea wasn't just tea.

10

I escaped from Esther, finding refuge within Larke House. It meant missing a talk by an academic from Colson College on "Object-oriented Ontology in Julia Larke's Oeuvre." I could live with that.

I moved through the gloomy Victorian mansion. The front entrance, with its double doors standing wide open, glowed like a rectangular sun.

Stepping outside, I closed my eyes against the bright light. I took a deep breath, filled my lungs, and then exhaled. What a relief to escape the constant chatter and the endless ream of academic jargon.

"You're way out of line," someone yelled.

I opened my eyes. At the bottom of the steps, Miranda engaged in a heated argument with a young man in a baseball cap. Not just any young man. It was my brother Scottie.

A handful of symposium guests, escapees like me, stood nearby and stared at the drama. One of the guests held a t-shirt in one hand and a mug in the other.

Scottie's cargo bike stood parked by the curb, and its cargo box—with the Scottie's Ice Cream Shop logo printed on the side—overflowed with merchandise. Poster tubes. T-shirts. Mugs. Even at this distance, I could see the t-shirts bore prints of Julia Larke paintings.

"Oh, great," I mumbled to myself as I hurried down the stairs. This old dispute again.

Miranda grabbed a t-shirt in a fist and shook it at Scottie.

"We had an agreement," she said. "I've called the cops."

"Calm down," Scottie said. "I didn't do anything wrong."

"Didn't do anything wrong? You've been selling Larke merchandise right under my nose—and when I've got the biggest event of the year."

As I joined them, Scottie looked over and frowned.

"Sis, stay out of this."

"I'm not meddling. Just reporting. But Mom's a different story."

I pointed at the police cruiser that came gliding down the street. Scottie groaned. The car pulled over to the curb and Mom stepped out on the passenger's side. On the driver's side, Deputy Douglas got out and shut the door behind him.

"What's the problem?" Mom asked Miranda.

"Scottie's selling merchandise again, despite what we agreed."

"Scottie, is this true?"

Scottie shrugged. "We agreed I could sell the last of my stock."

"And is this it?" Mom gestured at the cargo bike.

"Yup."

Miranda stepped in. "He said that last time, too. His final sale is endless. He keeps adding to the 'last of his stock.'"

"Miranda's overreacting," Scottie said. "Besides, it's not like I'm competing with her. She doesn't have a store yet."

"I do sell posters and t-shirts. When I can. And maybe if

you didn't keep stealing business from me, I'd have a chance to set up a proper store."

"You're making excuses."

"How dare you," Miranda spat, taking a step toward him. Fists clenched. Face flushed.

Mom stepped between them, and—yikes—for a second, I worried Miranda would take a swing at her. Miranda never lost her cool like this. The stress must be getting to her. To be fair, Scottie could stretch anyone's patience, and something about this 'last of my stock' business smelled fishy.

Mom said, "There's a simple solution to this. Why don't we take a ride down to your ice cream shop, Scottie, and we can all have a look at this stock of yours?" She turned to Miranda. "If you see that Scottie is finally out of stock, will that give you peace of mind?"

Miranda, her lips pressed shut, nodded.

"Come on then," Mom said. "I can give you a ride to the docks."

"I'll take my cargo bike," Scottie said.

Miranda narrowed her eyes. "He's going to hide it before we get there."

"Don't worry," Mom said. "We'll beat him to the shop. Besides, Scottie won't go inside until we get there." She gave Scottie her sternest look. "Will you, Scottie?"

Scottie mumbled, "No, Mom."

The little group disbanded. Scottie climbed onto his cargo bike. Miranda headed toward the cruiser with Deputy Douglas.

Mom gestured at me.

"Come along, Parker. This'll make a good story."

I hesitated for a moment. The entrance to Larke House still stood open. The lecture still underway. And after that, another lecture. I checked the time. A detour to Scottie's Ice

Cream Shop wouldn't take long. I dug out the program and checked the agenda. After the talk on object-oriented ontology and then the one on semiotics, the symposium would break for lunch. I'd have time to catch up with Teddy then. And Mom was right—local disputes like this one were perfect for *The Allington Gazette*. Dad would love it.

I turned my back on Larke House, feeling a little guilty at how relieved I was to go.

"Coming, Mom…"

11

Beneath the dock, the water splashed against the piles. Mom, Deputy Douglas, and Miranda walked ahead of me. We passed the Breeze, my brother Ray's restaurant and bar. Scottie, pulling his cargo bike, overtook me and then the others. His bike tires thumped against the wooden boards.

Scottie's Ice Cream Shop stood out, even among the other colorful dockside cafes and restaurants. It had a rainbow-striped awning and a giant ice-cream cone statue outside.

He parked the bike against the side of the shop. Miranda crossed her arms and watched him unlock the rolling shutters and then heave them up.

"This is good timing," he said to no one in particular. "I have to open in half an hour, anyway."

Jingling his keys, he unlocked the door to the shop and stepped inside. Miranda jumped forward, as if afraid he would bolt inside. But he didn't. He waited for us, holding open the door.

Inside, the cooler hummed. Empty tables stood ready

for this evening's guests. In summer, the shop would be open all day. But until Allington teemed with tourists, the ice-cream business would be slow. Scottie didn't worry. He was a serial entrepreneur with half a dozen side hustles. Business, he often told me, was only slow if you were.

Behind the glass, the frozen mounds looked enticing. Dark-brown chocolate. Light green pistachio. Creamy pink raspberry. A craving stirred in me. Maybe I'd have time to drop by and ask Scottie for an ice cream later tonight. Family members got a discount. Not a big one, of course. Scottie wasn't big on discounts, unless it drove bigger sales.

Scottie opened the back door and stood aside, so we could all file into the storage room. Boxes stood stacked against the wall. Waffle cones, paper cups, wooden spoons. Everything related to the ice cream business.

But a box on the floor bore the name of a printing company on the side: Canterbury Print.

Miranda flipped it open.

Inside lay a single t-shirt.

"See?" Scottie picked it up and revealed the design on the front: a reproduction of Larke's "Moon over Allington." He said, "I'm down to my last shirt. Except for what's in my cargo bike, of course."

Miranda frowned. "Fine."

A knock on the door and a man's voice hollering "hello" made us all turn toward the entrance.

"Excuse me," Scottie said.

He moved past us, hurrying through the shop. Out front, he spoke in a low, urgent voice to someone.

A man said, "Sure, I'm early. But so what? You ordered this stuff, didn't you?"

Mom gave me a look. I nodded. We both knew Scottie well enough to realize that he might be up to something.

Together, we headed out to the entrance, with Miranda and Deputy Douglas close behind.

Scottie propped open the door with his hip. A delivery guy stood next to a cart heaped with boxes. Each bore the same logo as on the box inside the shop: Canterbury Print.

"More t-shirts, Scottie?" Mom asked.

"Just the usual touristy stuff."

"Let's take a look." She turned to the delivery man. "Do you mind opening one of the boxes?"

The man shrugged, dug out a box cutter from his cargo pants, and then sliced open the top box. He peeled back the flaps and gestured for us to go ahead and look.

Mom reached into the box and pulled out a t-shirt. Then another. And another. She unfolded all three. Each revealed the same print: a big red heart and the classic message, "I love Allington."

"Told you so," Scottie said with a smile. "The usual touristy stuff."

Mom shoved the t-shirts back into the box and turned to Miranda.

"Satisfied?"

Miranda nodded. "Satisfied."

Mom reiterated to the two of them what the original agreement was: Scottie could sell the rest of his merchandise, but he must respect Miranda's exclusivity—and Larke House's copyright.

"You know you don't have the rights to these images," Mom said. "Technically, Miranda could sue you for damages."

"But I won't," Miranda said with a sigh. "I'd rather solve this in a practical way. Who wants to spend the next year wrangling with lawyers?"

"Good," Mom said. "Then everyone's happy."

Miranda nodded, and so did Scottie. Briefly. Then he got busy with the new t-shirts, guiding the delivery guy to the storage room in the back. Head down. No turning back to us.

In fact, was he avoiding my gaze?

I called out to him. "See you, Scottie. Maybe I'll stop by for ice cream later."

"Cool, see you later."

"Free ice cream for your baby sister?"

"Sure thing."

He waved at me from the door to the storage room, still not looking my way. When was the last time Scottie gave me anything for free? He was definitely being cagey. But why?

12

By the time I left Scottie's Ice Cream Shop, it was time for lunch. So I headed for Peony Lane and Cafe Larke. But I hesitated in the doorway, tempted to cross the street.

On the opposite corner of Peony and Main, the entrance to Balthazar Books stood open. Allington's independent bookstore. The books beckoned. Could I justify 10 minutes of book browsing? I sighed. I knew 10 minutes would quickly become an hour, and I only had a short break before I needed to go back to Larke House.

The walls inside Cafe Larke were painted bright yellow. Big purple letters on one wall said, "Have a Larke!" Plants hung from hooks in the ceiling and wooden shelves overflowed with books and knickknacks. The cafe had such a cozy feeling that it felt like a second home.

It was also an ode to Julia Larke. With the symposium underway, the posters of Julia Larke's artwork on the walls took on greater significance. I recognized a print of "Moon over Allington" and, after doing my homework and attending the talks, could name all the others, too: "Shady Grove" and "The Pullman Picnic" and "The Lumber Yard."

At the counter, Ashley, one of the cafe staff, stood alongside my sister Joy, who owned Cafe Larke. But the line was long, giving me time to think.

As I waited in line, I studied the prints. In the bright, cheerful cafe, the artwork added to the coziness. But across town, someone had murdered a man because of the art. Joe was small-time, but his murder wasn't. Somehow Knox Kensington was connected. But could Esther Winch's version of Knox be trusted? She wanted to smear his reputation, hoping I would print damaging rumors. Obviously, she had a chip on her shoulder. But was it more than that?

And in the end, who benefited from Joe's death? He'd failed to steal the painting. Which meant the killer might've saved it from disappearing into the underground art market. A scenario Miranda, in particular, was afraid of.

Aunt Lil's Larke painting might not be worth half a million, but if it was one of the best lake views, it could yield $3,000 at auction. Surely, Larke House could manage that. And if Miranda didn't have the money, would she kill Joe to stop him?

"No, that makes no sense," I told myself.

"What makes no sense? The falafel sandwich special?"

Teddy was standing next to me, grinning.

"Where did you come from?"

"Same place you came from."

"I didn't see you at the symposium this morning."

"Late night. I got there after things got started and I sat in the back."

"So you missed the 'Radical Domesticity' talk."

He laughed. "I think I'll survive."

"Yeah, I think you will. Did you eat lunch yet?"

"Nope—why do you think I skipped the line?" he said and winked.

We reached the counter. He leaned close to the glass, and I did, too, studying the food on display.

Ashley smiled at us. "What can I get you?"

Teddy and I ordered the same thing: hummus and grilled veggies on a ciabatta with a side of kale chips, plus a lemonade. We waited at the end of the counter for our food and drinks to be ready.

Joy brought it out. "Oh, hi, Teddy. Long time no see." She turned to me. "Dad tells me you're covering the Julia Larke symposium. You lucky duck."

Joy was the only person I knew who said "lucky duck" without any irony. She lived up to her name, radiating warmth, happiness, and openness. People sometimes thought it was because she practiced yoga—in fact, she owned the Pure Joy Yoga Studio—but I knew better: Joy had always been filled with joy. Running a cozy cafe and teaching yoga simply suited her personality.

Outside, the sun was shining. Couples wandered up the pedestrian-only Peony Lane. All along the cobblestone street were shops and cafes and restaurants. Most seats outside Cafe Larke were taken, but luckily there was a table free, and Teddy and I sat down.

"What a gorgeous day," he said, squinting up at the sun. "And what a gorgeous town."

"Do you miss it?" I asked him.

"Sometimes."

Our food and drinks arrived. I bit into my hummus sandwich. The veggies exploded with fresh flavor, grilled but still crispy, and the hummus was rich and creamy.

Then Teddy said, "All right, honestly? I often miss Allington."

"But you haven't been back much, have you?"

He shrugged. "Life gets in the way."

He ate his sandwich. There was something he wasn't telling me.

"And…?"

"Jeez, Park, you're worse than a therapist."

We both laughed.

Then he grew serious. "The truth is I can only stand visits to my parents in small doses. I used to come back in summers to work at the family business. Already after the first week, I'd be desperate to leave. My dad's lectures about what makes a man, well, they drive me nuts. And my mom's platitudes are even worse. 'Hard work always pays off.' 'Money can't buy happiness.' 'Everything happens for a reason.'" He looked at me. "Don't you feel that way about your mom and dad sometimes?"

I shrugged. It felt awkward to tell the truth—that my mom, dad, and I loved each other and got along well. So well, in fact, that I'd moved back into my old bedroom at Broadstairs House. Right down the hallway from Scottie and Joy's rooms. Only my oldest siblings Amy and Ray lived elsewhere in Allington.

Teddy said, "Anyway, your mom doesn't say stuff like, 'Everything happens for a reason.'"

"Maybe everything does happen for a reason."

"You believe that?"

I shook my head. Lots of things didn't happen for a reason. But then an image flashed across my mind: Joe Rudder lying on the floor of the lounge. His death had happened for a reason, that was for sure.

Teddy went on, "Things happen for a reason, and that reason is people. People make things happen. I left Allington because my parents sent me to boarding school.

That was their choice, not mine. I became a writer because I wouldn't major in business like they told me to. I wouldn't take over the family locksmith business. My choice, not theirs. I stayed away from Allington because they're still here. Also my choice." Hunched over, he scowled at his sandwich. "One day they'll be gone. Maybe then I'll move back to Allington and live happily ever after in a big mansion on Chestnut Hill."

I didn't quite know what to say.

But then Teddy straightened up and smiled, breaking the awkward moment. "Enough of that. Therapy session over. Let's talk about what happened yesterday instead. I mean, wow."

"Yeah, wow."

I filled him in on the marble bust under the table, the footprint on the rug, and the discoveries in Joe Rudder's room.

Teddy sighed. "I wish I could've been there."

"I'm sorry you weren't."

He eyed me for a moment, as if he was making up his mind about something.

"Truth?"

"Truth."

"I was pretty angry that your mom cut me out. This is my story, too. My town, too. I have a right to it as much as you do. Just because you're a Lee doesn't give you special privileges."

"I know."

What else could I say? Mom's decision to include me in the investigation was nepotism. No two ways about it. But if I questioned her choices, I knew exactly what she'd say. She'd say she trusted Dad. She trusted me. She knew we'd help, not hinder, the investigation. And in the end, to her, the only thing that mattered was the investigation.

But I also knew what Teddy would say. He'd say he could be trusted, too. I couldn't argue with that. Despite losing touch with him over the years, he was one of my oldest friends.

Still, it was Mom's call to make.

I changed the topic. "What do you know about Joe Rudder?"

"What makes you think I know anything about him?"

"Well, you're like an encyclopedia of the art scene. I assumed you might've heard something."

"All right, I heard something." He still sounded sore. But after another bite, he added, "I've seen him snooping around art events before. People know him as a scavenger—someone who looks through old ladies' attics. Then, finding something valuable, he tells them he'll gladly take their junk off their hands. Like he's doing them a favor. Maybe he pays them. Maybe he doesn't."

"Sounds morally dubious."

"Yeah, 'morally dubious' sums up Joe Rudder. Actually, I heard a rumor that he started out in the art world at a gallery or auction house. Something like that. But he got sticky fingers around all those valuables, and he was told to leave."

"Interesting. Very interesting."

I flipped open my notebook and jotted down:

Joe Rudder's professional background???

Maybe Mom had already done the research—or Deputy Douglas had.

Teddy smiled. "Look at us. You're like me—totally addicted to sensational stories."

"Guilty as charged."

We both laughed, and it felt good. It released something. Restored something.

Teddy took another big bite of his sandwich. I drank my lemonade.

He said, "Hey, do me a favor? Don't cut me out of this story again. I'll share everything I know or discover, if you'll do the same. Deal?"

I smiled. "Deal."

13

Back at Larke House, Teddy abandoned me to a group of academics by the coffee station. They were discussing modernism, post-modernism, and post-post-modernism. Up on stage, a speaker droned on about the organizational evolution of art colonies in the U.S.

I jotted down notes I'd never read again and looked around for someone to save me.

Miranda stood near the back entrance to Larke House, drinking a cup of coffee.

I grabbed a coffee and fled to her. "Happy with how things are going?"

"Yes," she said. "I think so. I hope so."

"No disasters, as far as I can see."

"What do you call a murder?"

"Free publicity?"

She grimaced. "Larke House has a lot riding on this symposium, and the whole debacle with Joe Rudder looks bad."

"You've invested a lot of money?"

"Yes, that. But it's also our reputation—and Julia Larke's.

We've attracted an unusual amount of attention, and I feel like we have this one shot to convert skeptics into believers."

"From what I hear, Julia Larke's reputation is already rising—as are the prices at auctions."

"Sure. But there's still a lot of resistance in academia, and among the old guard at the auction houses."

"For example, Knox Kensington."

"Yes, for example."

"Tell me more about him."

"Knox Kensington? He comes from a distinguished academic background, and an even more distinguished, upper crust New England family. He's built a reputation as an expert. A man of impeccable taste. A bellwether for the art market."

"So it's a big deal that he's here."

Miranda nodded. "A really big deal."

I told her about Knox denying any knowledge of Joe Rudder and then Esther claiming he was a liar.

Miranda said, "Don't believe everything she says. She likes to stir things up. In fact, if Esther saw a hornet's nest, she'd jab a stick in it."

A guy wearing a Larke House Staff t-shirt interrupted us. He reminded Miranda that the afternoon's sessions would end shortly. Miranda excused herself, hurrying off with her colleague.

I leaned against the wall, drinking my own cup of coffee. The speaker on stage droned on. I heard the words, and the words made sense, but what was his point?

Another speaker came on. She was no more understandable. She lectured on "The Semantics of Color: Words as Image and Image as Words in late American Impressionism." My head spun with all the new jargon.

Finally, mercifully, Miranda took to the stage and thanked all the participants.

"A practical matter," she then said. "Due to tragic events at the Lakeview Inn, our venue for tonight's dinner will be relocated. In an hour, we'll meet for pre-dinner drinks at the Lake Breeze Brewery, followed by dinner. It's a delightful, local brewery and restaurant down on the docks—I'm sure you'll love it. Thank you all."

Applause from the audience, which sounded like dying hands clapping. Everyone must be as exhausted as I was. Because it couldn't be about the change of venue. People loved the Breeze, including visitors to town. I felt bad for Aunt Lil losing the business while the crime was under investigation, but at least the symposium guests would go to my brother Ray's brewery instead.

"Well, honestly..." Esther Winch said behind me. She was coming out of Larke House, accompanying another academic. "A brewery? You can't expect people to pay good money to attend a symposium on an important American artist, and then downgrade their dinner to bar food."

The two stationed themselves in the doorway.

"Miranda's made a mess of things..." Esther shook her head. "She simply doesn't have the expertise..."

Charming. Esther might specialize in Julia Larke, but her side hustle was ragging on Miranda. The rivalry between the two must go deep. Esther continued to bad mouth Miranda and her symposium, and after a while, I couldn't stand it anymore.

I squeezed past Esther and her friend and headed for the exit.

On my way down the front steps, an idea occurred to me. Maybe Esther somehow had a connection to Joe Rudder's death. But how did killing Joe relate to badmouthing Miranda and Knox?

Halfway down the steps, I stopped. Scottie stood by the curb. Once again, his cargo bike was overflowing with Julia Larke t-shirts. A cluster of symposium guests stood around him, handing him cash for the merchandise.

Scottie, smiling, looked up. His smile died when he saw me. He quickly handed a customer his change. Then shoved the t-shirts into the cargo box and swung up on the saddle.

"Hey," a woman said. "I wanted to buy one too."

"Uh, tomorrow," Scottie said.

He kicked off from the curb and pedaled down Chestnut Hill. Before turning onto a side street, he glanced back. As if checking on me.

Was he wondering what I'd seen? Well, I'd seen him sell t-shirts, but wasn't that the agreement he had with Miranda? That he could sell the rest of his stock?

Although...

That cargo bike looked surprisingly full.

14

"**A**rt X *is going to be the first and greatest art museum on the moon.*"

My oldest brother Ray, co-owner of the Lake Breeze Brewery with his wife, Roxie, glanced up at the TV. "Is he serious?"

I shook my head. "He's crazy enough to do it. And rich enough."

I sat on a stool at the Breeze's hardwood bar, watching the TV set overhead while I sipped the Breeze's wheat beer. An interviewer was talking to billionaire Arthur X. He was going to build an art museum on the moon—called "Art X" —and fill it with his private collection.

"*But who's going to be able to visit your art museum?*"

"*Space travel is becoming easier by the day.*"

"*But the average person—*"

Arthur X smiled. "*The average person will remain average —and down on earth.*"

"That's all I can take." Ray raised the remote control and hit the off button. The screen turned black. "Does money make people crazy? Or is it that crazy people are great at making money?"

"Money definitely makes them do extreme things," I said. I remembered something. "You know the man who died? Joe Rudder. He was reading Arthur X's memoir about his art collecting."

"Amazingly, it's a bestseller," Ray said. "The guy's toxic. I'll never understand why some people love him."

All around me, symposium guests were chatting. Glasses clinking. Music playing. Someone approached me, hovering out of the corner of my eye. As if waiting.

A moment later, Miranda slipped onto the stool next to mine.

"Men like Arthur X..." She didn't finish her sentence. She took a deep breath, as if preparing herself for something difficult. Then said, "You mentioned Joe Rudder. Well, I knew him."

I swiveled my stool toward her. "You did?"

Why hadn't I asked her? Knox had been such a distraction. Esther, too. But of course I should've asked Miranda.

"Did you know him well?"

She shook her head. "He'd snooped around Allington before, looking for art or antiques he could snap up. A couple paintings that might've been original Larkes fell into his hands, and he sold them on the black market. But I can't prove any wrongdoing."

"You knew he was here in Allington?"

"Yes, I saw him at the inn. I should've come right out and told you, but then I didn't and now I feel awkward about it. Like I was keeping a secret."

I understood the feeling. Innocent little facts could become heavy burdens when we kept them secret. Still, could Miranda gain anything by keeping this knowledge secret? If so, I couldn't figure it out.

"Why do you think he was here?"

"I assumed he came back because Julia Larke's paintings have been increasing in value. More and more big collectors want to buy her art. Maybe he thought he'd find something."

"Maybe he did."

I dug out my phone and showed Miranda the pictures I'd taken of the canvases in Joe Rudder's hotel room.

"I'd have to study them in person," she said, holding the phone up to her face, squinting at the screen. "But my first impression? I'd guess these were copies. Good copies. Maybe done by one of Larke's students under her supervision."

"What's the chance they were variations done by Larke herself?"

"There's a chance. There's always a chance. As with the one your aunt found in the attic, I need to examine the technique to determine who painted them. When the symposium ends, I'll have the time and headspace to take a look."

I took my phone back. "Look, Miranda. This is urgent. Joe Rudder probably died because of that painting."

"Or for some other reason," she said. "I've got a lot on my plate..."

"The killer may still be at the symposium. If the painting is a genuine Larke, it may tell us something about why Joe was murdered—and maybe also who did it."

"And if it's a copy?" Esther said from behind us. "What does that tell you?"

I cringed. Her again. She was like a bad penny, always turning up. Didn't she have anything better to do?

She said, "No need to fret over those paintings, Miranda.

I'll gladly assess them. After all, I have the necessary expertise."

"And I don't?"

She smirked. "I didn't say that."

"Miranda's input is important," I said.

Esther ignored me. "I'll take a look at the painting first thing in the morning. Then we'll know for certain if it's real or fake. See you at the inn bright and early."

As Esther walked away, Miranda hissed, "Snake."

"A second opinion isn't a bad thing," I said, pretending to be preoccupied with my beer. As I took a swig, I glanced at Miranda out of the corner of my eye. I said, "But if you want to leave it to Esther, I totally understand..."

Miranda's face turn dark with anger. She clenched her jaw.

"Second opinion?" she spat. "Are you saying my opinion is secondary?"

I nearly fell off my stool. If she'd punched me then, I wouldn't have been surprised. It wasn't like Miranda to fly into a rage...

"Hey," I said, "I wasn't suggesting—"

"I'll be damned if I'll let Esther Winch walk around my town and decide what's a Larke and what isn't. She has no right. No right."

Miranda jerked her drink to her mouth and drained the glass, then slammed it down on the bar. She gestured for Ray to get her another.

Then took a deep, shuddering breath. And let it out.

"Oh, rats." She pinched the bridge of her nose. Turning to me, she put a hand on my arm and said, "I'm so sorry. That was uncalled for. I'm hungry. I'm tired. And I've had it up to here with Esther Winch."

"No problem. I get it."

And I did. It wasn't like Miranda to fly off the handle like that. Though she'd done it a couple of times now. So maybe...

I studied Miranda as she gulped her second glass of wine.

How much anger was building up inside her? And what did a full eruption look like?

15

The next morning, I walked into the lounge at the Lakeview Inn with an uninvited guest: Teddy.

Mom raised a questioning eyebrow.

"Teddy's been following Julia Larke's rise in popularity," I said. "He may be helpful."

She gave me a long look. I met her gaze, showing her how serious I was. I'd made a promise, and as far as I was concerned, Teddy and I were a team. She gave me a single nod, accepting my decision. Trusting me.

Mom turned to Miranda and Esther.

"Are we all set?" she asked.

"I think so," Miranda said.

"I certainly am," Esther said.

The two Larke-like variations of the lake view, which we'd found in Joe Rudder's room, stood on a loveseat. Next to them, on an armchair, sat Aunt Lil's painting. It had been released from forensics.

This was the first time I could study them side by side. Superficially, they were the same: the lake, the little island, the clear blue sky. No other details to set them apart, except maybe a variation in color. Even the brushstroke technique looked the same, though an expert might disagree.

Miranda and Esther each held a magnifying glass to the painting, studying the brushstrokes.

While they worked, Mom turned to me and Teddy and explained the "inconclusive" forensics results.

She said, "Too many fingerprints to make sense of. And the Marie Antoinette bust was clean. Which suggests the killer wore gloves. And given how many symposium guests milled through this room, the DNA evidence is useless."

"So we've got nothing?" I asked.

"No, we do have something. You were right. Joe Rudder's shoes had no ashes on the bottom. The footprint may belong to the killer."

I thought about that. "Which means the killer stepped onto the hearth—to do what? Steal the painting? But then things may have happened in a different order. Could Joe have interrupted the killer?" I shook my head. "That doesn't make sense. Because the killer left the painting behind."

Teddy said, "These two look like Larke paintings to me. What about the one from the attic?"

Miranda took one of the canvasses we'd found in Joe Rudder's room and turned it over. She said, "Often Larke would write on the back, adding a date or comment. Sometimes she'd even attach a sketch she made of her subject before attempting the painting. Here. Look. There's nothing."

"But more importantly," Esther said, "the brushstrokes."

"Yes, the brushstrokes," Miranda said.

"This is a point on which Miranda and I have often disagreed."

"There's one disputed painting—Larke's 'The Goat'—

which I believe she painted only once. The original is the one at Larke House."

"And I," Esther said, "know with 100 percent certainty that the so-called 'Philadelphia Goat' is a second iteration Larke created in the summer of 1912. The brush strokes confirm it."

Miranda shook her head. "We know from the diaries of her student, Millicent Hadley, that Larke used 'The Goat' as the subject for their lessons. And Millicent had an uncanny ability to mimic Larke's brushstrokes."

"Uncanny? You can still tell the difference. Or at least, I can. But then you've had your slip-ups in the past, Miranda, and—"

"Enough," Mom said. "Save your squabbles for later. What can you tell us about these paintings?"

"All three were made by the same artist," Esther said.

Miranda nodded. "Without a doubt."

Clear agreement between Miranda and Esther. No bickering. No second-guessing.

"Teddy thinks they're original Larkes," I said, and Teddy nodded. "Do you?"

Esther shook her head. "No."

Miranda agreed. "No. All three paintings were done by the same person. Clearly no amateur, but definitely not Larke. These are copies."

"Very good copies," Esther added. "Likely a student of hers, working closely with their mentor. Though not Millicent Hadley."

"No, I agree. This wasn't Millicent. Probably a later student, working in a studio. That is, he or she copied from a Larke canvas instead of painting the actual lake view."

I stared at her, amazed. "So Joe Rudder was killed over a painting that's only worth—"

"Fifty bucks," Esther said, "if you're lucky."

16

Outside on the back porch, I leaned against the railing. Teddy stood next to me. Aunt Lil next to him. The breeze off the lake ruffled my hair. Out on the island in the lake, the trees rippled in the wind. A bird banked into the wind and then dove into the water.

The view was the one Julia Larke had painted. The one her student had then copied. I took a deep breath, relishing the clean air.

"I'm sorry," Teddy said to Aunt Lil. "You must be disappointed."

"Why?" Aunt Lil said. "I love the painting for its subject, not the artist. This student's work is still wonderful."

I tried to match my aunt's positivity. "And since most of Larke's students were locals, it still counts as local artwork."

"There you go," Aunt Lil said. "So I'm happy. Although I'm disappointed about my blanket."

"What blanket?" I asked.

"A nice wool blanket that's gone missing from the lounge. It was on the armchair. Now it's gone." She rubbed her neck, her bangles jangling on her wrists. "If it didn't sound so ridiculous, I'd say the killer stole my blanket."

"Maybe the killer thought your blanket was worth more than the painting," Teddy said with a glint in his eye.

"Now you're teasing me. But seriously. It would've been something to have a real Julia Larke hanging over my fireplace. I wouldn't sell it to the highest bidder. It doesn't seem right. A Julia Larke painting belongs at Larke House. It belongs in Allington." She shook her head. "Like my wool blanket belongs in my lounge."

Teddy said, "Nobody would judge you, if you wanted to sell a valuable painting."

"Well, not so valuable," I cut in, "if we're talking dollars and cents."

He continued: "Julia's own father cut down half of the Allington Woods and exported the timber. He didn't worry about whether the trees belonged in Allington or not."

Lil raised an eyebrow. "And is the lesson, young man, that Mr. Larke did the right thing?"

"In school, we were taught he was a hero. He made Allington rich. It's part of our history."

"You're right—it is part of our history," Aunt Lil said, and then gestured out at the lake and tree-covered banks beyond. "But I can tell you this: these woods pulse with nature's mysteries. If I owned them, I wouldn't cut them down. I wouldn't simply repeat history."

The door to the lounge opened and Mom stepped out to join us. She'd sent Esther and Miranda down to the police station with Deputy Douglas, so he could take their official statements on the paintings.

She leaned on the railing next to me, looking out at the lake, the little island, and the woods beyond. In the distance, the Lake Allington Resort & Spa nestled among the trees on the far shore, its white roofs shining in the sunlight.

Mom said, "Why would someone kill Joe Rudder to stop him from stealing a worthless painting?"

"Maybe the killer didn't know it was worthless," Teddy suggested.

"Maybe Joe didn't either," I said, building on what Teddy had said. "And then a rival thief interrupted his attempt to steal the painting, and they fought. Or the reverse: Joe interrupted the rival thief."

"But then why leave the painting behind?" Mom asked.

"The killer panicked," I said. "Remember, the alarm was going off. More than a hundred people stood right out here on the porch. The killer could've planned to grab the painting and run. They'd count on having just enough time to dash for the other door and run out through the reception."

"That makes sense," Teddy said. "Then Joe interrupts the attempt. They struggle. The killer grabs the bust and whacks Joe over the head, and then, hearing someone at the door to the porch—"

"The killer makes a run for it."

Mom said, "That sounds like the most sensible explanation."

Still, something wasn't adding up. We were missing a piece of the puzzle.

I gazed out at the lake. The rippling waters, the little island, and the bird I spotted earlier, now out of the water, resting on the inn's dock.

The bird...

"Unless..."

"Unless what?" Mom asked.

"Unless there weren't three paintings. But four."

My heart beat faster. That was it. The missing piece.

I looked at Aunt Lil, then at Teddy, and finally at Mom, who nodded for me to go on.

I said, "When I first saw the painting in the attic, when Joe insisted he get 'first dibs' on it—that time, I noticed something. A detail in the painting, one that set it apart from the two canvases we found in Joe Rudder's room. There was a bird in the sky."

"So?" Mom said.

"So, this morning when I looked at the three paintings— the ones Miranda and Esther agree were created by the same artist—well, I noticed something. They were all the same. There's a lake and the little island and a blue sky. They all have an identical blue sky. No clouds. Nothing. Just blue."

Mom raised her eyebrows. "And no bird, either?"

"Right. No bird."

"Which means..."

She grabbed my shoulder and gave it a squeeze. "Which means," she said, excited, "Lil's painting in the attic was an original Larke. The one with the bird in the sky. And the killer took it."

17

Mom left for the police station, Teddy headed to Larke House for the symposium, and with her lounge no longer a crime scene, Aunt Lil had plenty of hotel work to see to. She went inside.

But I stayed on the porch, leaning against the railing. I needed to leave for the symposium soon. But I wasn't ready to dive back into academia just yet. As I gazed out at the lake, I let my mind drift over the events of the past few days.

My heart did a little backflip.

I'd spotted him again. The man in the rowboat.

I straightened up.

This time he didn't have the benefit of the mist to cover his progress. And this time he wasn't heading back from Gull Island—he was heading toward it. And fast. Pulling at the oars with such force that the boat flew over waves, the prow splashing into the water.

Intuition rang like an alarm, raising the little hairs on my neck.

First the mystery man on the lake. Then Joe Rudder's

death and the theft of the Julia Larke painting. Were they coincidences?

I looked around for someone to do something. But I was alone. Down the steps from the back porch lay the inn's dock. And four rowboats tethered to the piles.

I bounded down the steps. As quickly as I could, I untied the rope to one of my aunt's rowboats and jumped in. I pushed off from the dock.

The rowboat slid into the lake. I grabbed the oars and lowered them into the water and pulled. Within moments, I was gliding past the dock and out onto the open lake.

Soon, I was huffing as I pulled on the oars. My arms ached. My back, too. But I kept hauling at the oars. And hauling. And hauling.

After what felt like an eternity, the sandy bottom became visible in the water. Then the rowboat bumped against a tree reaching out from the little island. No other boats in sight. The mystery man must've rowed around to the other side.

The trees clung to the banks of the island, their roots half in, half out of water. Like many others, the tree nearest to me leaned over the water, providing me with a makeshift dock.

I tied up the boat. Then reached up and grabbed a branch, huffing and puffing as I dragged myself up.

I tiptoed into the thicket that grew on the island. I pushed aside thorny brambles and ducked below low-hanging branches, careful not to make too much noise.

The old cabin was back there. It must be where the man was hiding. If he really was hiding...

Rounding a tree, I stopped. In front of me, the trees parted, and in the clearing stood the cabin.

The wood cabin was a ruin. It had once had two stories,

but the roof was gone, leaving the second floor open to the sky. As a kid, I'd spent many happy hours exploring this cabin. With Teddy, too. The two of us sitting on the second floor of the cabin and sharing a lukewarm bottle of coke, feet dangling over the edge...

A scraping sound came from within the cabin.

"He's inside," I muttered to myself.

I tiptoed toward the cabin door, which stood open. In fact, it was falling off its rusted hinges. I slipped inside.

Inside to the right, rickety stairs led up to a trapdoor and, beyond that, the second floor. Next to the stairs, a man crouched down by a weather-proof crate. It was a modern object in a room full of old detritus. Dried leaves. Twigs. Empty bottles with faded labels. And some new ones, too—signs that teenagers were still hanging out on the island.

The man rummaged in the crate.

I stepped toward him and stopped, my heart leaping into my throat. A snake squirmed under my foot. I half-stifled a cry.

Snake Island. That was what Teddy called this place—and didn't he say he thought he saw a—?

Snake. That wasn't a snake.

Under my foot, the snake had transformed into an old piece of half-rotten rope. It was never a snake. Just my imagination. But the man had heard me and he spun around.

Seeing me, his eyes went wide.

"Park?"

I stared at my brother. "Scottie?"

18

"What in the world are you doing?"

I stepped forward and Scottie held up his hands, trying to block me from seeing what was in the crate.

"This is none of your business, sis…"

I ducked around him, outmaneuvering him to the left.

"Hey," he protested.

The crate, behind him, contained a pile of t-shirts, poster tubes, and boxes with mugs. I pulled out a t-shirt and unfolded it. The t-shirt said, "Julia Larke." A reproduction of "Moon over Allington" filled the front.

"Scott Lee," I said, doing my best impression of Mom when she was unimpressed. "Care to explain this?"

He groaned. "I know, I know, I know."

I opened a tube and pulled out a poster of Larke's "Mother and Child," one of her most popular paintings. "Clearly, you don't know," I said. "Didn't you and Miranda come to an agreement about merchandise?"

He looked down at his feet. "We kinda did."

"But you ordered more," I said. "What did you do, replenish your stock every day, a little at a time?"

He nodded. "I've only been filling my cargo bike. I've tried to keep as little as possible in my storage room."

"Because you knew Miranda might demand to see your stock." I thought back to Mom's inspection of Scottie's Ice Cream Shop. "And the delivery that came when we dropped by...?"

"I got lucky," he said. "Mom opened one of the boxes with the regular shirts, not the Julia Larke prints. If she'd opened all the boxes, she would've found them. Along with mugs and posters."

"Jeez, Scottie. Just to sell a few t-shirts and stuff."

"A man's gotta eat," he snapped.

"You're hardly living on the edge of poverty," I said. "In fact, you're living at home with your parents."

"All the more reason to grow my financial assets, so that one day, I can build some equity."

"You lied—you broke your promise to Miranda."

"I didn't lie. Not really."

I raised an eyebrow. "Not really? Kinda?"

He took the merchandise out of my hands, stuffing them back into the crate. "Look, it's unfair I can't sell what I want. Yesterday, I almost sold all my stock. I was lucky another delivery came the same day. You know what that shows?"

I said, "That this was a premeditated crime?"

"No," Scottie said, frowning. "It shows there's a market for my merchandise. People love it. There's demand, but no supply. I'm doing folks a favor. I'm doing what's natural. I'm doing—"

"Come on, Scottie, admit it: you're doing what you want, regardless of the consequences for others."

"You're making me out to be a villain."

I lifted my foot and kicked the crate shut.

"You're not a villain," I said. "But you're being unfair to Miranda. It's her job to take care of Julia Larke's legacy. Running Larke House is part of that, and by stealing copyrighted images and printing them on merchandise for profit, you're making her job harder."

"Stealing," he mumbled, "is a harsh word."

"I'll leave the technical terms to Mom..."

He chewed his lip. "You don't have to tell her about this, do you?"

"Are you going to talk to Miranda? Are you going to get rid of this stock and stop selling illegal merchandise?"

He glanced at the crate longingly. Then let out a sigh. "I guess I will..."

"Kinda? Not really?"

"No, I will. Really."

I smiled. "Then I don't think we need to involve Mom."

I watched Scottie carry the crate to his rowboat and helped him lift it aboard. I put a foot on the prow of his boat and shoved off. He grabbed the oars and began to row. Slowly this time. Nothing like the energetic pull I'd seen from afar. He bent over the oars, like a man defeated.

But I wasn't worried about Scottie. He'd bounce back. He always did. Right now, I was more concerned about my own disappointment. I'd hoped for a clue to Joe Rudder's murder. But no such luck.

I headed back across the island toward my own boat, pushing my way through the brambles. Trying not to feel too disappointed.

At the water's edge, I shimmied out onto the low-hanging tree and dropped into the rowboat. I untied the rope, grabbed the oars, and started rowing. All the while thinking through this latest discovery.

Since the mystery man had turned out to be Scottie, I'd have to look for clues to the murder someplace else. And where was most logical? At the symposium, of course.

The symposium. Oh, shoot. What time was it?

I stopped rowing, dug out my phone, and checked the time—and cursed when I saw how late I was for the symposium.

Plus, there was a message from Dad on my lock screen:

> I need the first article on the symposium before lunch time.

I groaned. I didn't want to disappoint Dad. After all, hiring me after I lost my job as a journalist in the big city was more of a favor than a smart financial move.

How was I going to keep up with the symposium, the merchandising dispute, and the murder, and still find time to write about it all?

The Allington Gazette occupied a former firehouse, a charming red-brick facade with tall ceilings inside. The instant I stepped inside, Dad stopped typing on his typewriter.

My dad had this thing about analog technology—turntable with vinyl at home, vintage typewriters at work—and I used to think it was crazy. But after moving back home, I'd begun to appreciate it.

His own preference was for a teal green Olivetti Studio 44. Mine was a candy red Royal Quiet de Luxe.

"Great. You're early. Then you'll have time to get me three reports: one on the symposium, the other on the murder, and the third on the dispute between Larke House and your brother."

I bit my lip. Dad leaned back in his chair, hands folded over his ample belly, and regarded me with those gentle basset hound eyes of his. "Are three reports too much?"

"No, of course not."

Dad didn't invoke fear in me. But he'd offered me a job when I most needed it, and I couldn't let him down.

I plopped down on my seat at the other messy desk. Which had once belonged to my dad. The newspaper office was big, the firehouse's tall ceilings providing lots of air and light. But like many other local newspapers, *The Gazette* was in decline. Dad and I were the only full-time journalists.

I moved aside old papers and fed a fresh sheet of paper into my typewriter. Then opened my laptop, which sat next to it. We didn't entirely live in the past at *The Gazette*.

I noticed an email from the Allington Police Department. The subject line simply said, "Important." Was it the forensics report? Some new lead in the case? I double clicked the message.

```
SUBJECT: Important


Sweetie, before you come home today,
could you please pick up the following
at the market:


  • Zucchini
  • Eggplant
  • Carrots
  • Bell peppers
  • Baby spinach
  • 1 can of diced tomatoes
  • Cottage cheese
  • Mozzarella cheese
  • Lasagna noodles


I'm forcing your dad to make his
famous lasagna for us. No need to buy
fixings for salad.
```

```
Love,

Mom
```

I sighed.

"Hey, Dad..."

"Is this about lasagna?"

"Yup."

"Already got the memo, thanks."

Since my inbox contained no other "important" messages, I turned back to my typewriter and jumped right into writing the report on the symposium.

Click-clack-clack. Across from me, Dad was typing, too. Click-clack-clack. The sound reverberated in the rafters high above us.

Now and then, I checked my notebook for details. In journalism school, I had a professor who taught us how to structure as we investigated. It had served me well in the big city, where the reporting beat had been fast paced. Even as I interviewed people or did research, I would structure—and restructure—the article. Sometimes in my head. Other times on paper. So by the time I sat down to write, I knew exactly how to approach the story. That allowed me to dive right in today.

After I'd drafted the symposium story, I moved on to the murder. I'd learned by trial and error that when I was putting down the first version, it was best to type as much as possible in one sitting. Then I could turn to revising afterward.

The words flew across the screen. The death of Joe Rudder and the suspicion that an original Julia Larke was missing flowed out of me.

But when I turned my attention to writing about Larke

House and Scottie, my typing slowed, the words jerked forward, leaping down the wrong track.

I tore the paper out of the typewriter, balled it up, and tossed it into the wastepaper basket.

"This story…" I gritted my teeth. "It feels like I only have half the facts."

"Oh?" Dad stopped typing and looked up at me. "The murder story?"

"No, I've got a full report on that. I don't have all the answers, but—"

"But a news story doesn't answer everything, only the lead."

"Right. The thing is, though, the conflict between Miranda and Scottie, it feels…incomplete."

"Incomplete?"

"Scottie's unhappy and so is Miranda. There ought to be a way both can get what they want without hurting each other."

"Sounds utopian. But if they're both willing to compromise, maybe it's not such a crazy idea."

I nodded. That was it: the story was missing a resolution to the conflict itself. Without that resolution, the story felt too small to matter. Too small to be published. And somehow small-minded and petty.

"I think we should wait," I said. "Hold off on the merchandise story."

"Hold off?"

I couldn't read Dad's expression. Did he disapprove of my suggestion?

"It's not because I'm trying to put off writing the article," I explained.

It was true. Why put off writing? If I had a story, I'd put

down the words and meet the deadline. Simple as that. I'd done it countless times before.

"And it's not because he's your brother?"

I snorted. "You mean am I trying to protect his fragile ego? Hardly. It's just that I think we can get a satisfying ending to this story if we wait. But if we publish it now, the story will be half-baked."

He raised an eyebrow. "And?"

"And…" I rubbed my neck. Would he think my reason for not wanting to do the story sounded silly? I took a chance and said, "Right now, the story's sensational. And ugly. It's about two Allingtonians at each other's throats."

"That sounds like a dramatic story. Won't readers love it?"

"They'll read it. But 'love' doesn't seem like the right word…"

"Then what is the right word?"

I thought about that for a while. "My first thought was *small-minded*," I finally said. "But *dirty* also describes it. It'll make them feel dirty. Or resentful."

"So what? Aren't we trying to sell newspapers? If you're right and they'll read the story, then we've succeeded." There was a twinkle in Dad's eyes. "Or have we?"

I shook my head. "Not if it makes people in Allington dislike each other. This is our town. If we're spreading resentment, sooner or later that's like pouring poison onto our own flower bed."

"Oh, I like that: *pouring poison onto our own flower bed*."

"I don't think it's our job to do that."

"All right. Then what is our job?"

That was harder to answer. "To tell stories…"

"What kinds of stories?"

"To tell the stories that help Allington…"

I was going to say "blossom," but it sounded so hokey.

Dad was watching me.

I sighed and said, "All right. Stories that help Allington blossom."

Dad smiled. He went back to typing.

"Sounds like you've got it under control," he said. Without looking up, he added, "Hold on the merchandise story, but give me your drafts of the murder and the symposium reports."

Warmth filled me. It was like having a respected professor praise my work. But different, too. I ran a hand along the edge of the desk. The desk my predecessors had worked at for so many years. This was an old newspaper with origins in the 1800s, and from its first year until now, it had been a family business. Generations of small-town journalists serving the community.

When I left for the city, I'd convinced myself I was done with Allington. What opportunities were there in such a small town? *The Gazette* couldn't give me the experience I was looking for. But I was beginning to see just how wrong I'd been.

I got back to work. I revised the two stories—the murder and the symposium—and handed them to Dad for his comments.

Then grabbed my messenger bag and got up. I turned back to him.

"Thanks, Dad," I said. "I'll be at Larke House, if you need me."

He waved, but he was bent over his typewriter, click-clack-clacking away. The beat following me all the way to the door. I felt a spring in my step, an excitement about the work I was doing.

Yeah, life in Allington—and work at *The Gazette*—might not be for everyone. But it suited me just fine.

20

"Things are getting interesting," Teddy said.

"What's going on?"

"Wait and see."

All around us, people were whispering. On stage, Miranda grabbed the microphone. She confirmed a change to the agenda, which sent a thrill rippling through the symposium crowd. Then Knox Kensington joined her, and the audience drew in a collective breath.

He walked on stage with the straight-backed authority of an aristocrat.

"He didn't even want to come," Teddy said. "And now he's speaking."

"Why the change of heart?"

Teddy shrugged. "Do we care? The story just got juicier."

As Knox began to speak—with everyone gazing in awe at him—Miranda walked off stage, glancing back at Knox with a frown on her face. What did this sudden change mean for her?

Knox spoke about American impressionism. He spoke about the connections between French artists and American. And finally, he mentioned Julia Larke, almost with a resigned sigh. But at this point his speech veered away from the academic.

"At Bishop & Company, we're committed to treating artistic legacy with respect. We believe that the seller should get the best possible deal. But art should also remain accessible to the public via museums. The two are not mutually exclusive."

A murmur spread through the audience.

This mention of commercialism must be unconventional. Why was Knox Kensington—of all people—talking about money at a symposium that had been so far removed from such considerations?

He went on. "Of course, there are private buyers—millionaires and billionaires with plenty of means—who can provide sellers with more cash in hand. At Bishop & Company, we offer a platform for sellers to get high prices while ensuring that the sale respects the true value of the artwork—and the legacy of the artist."

Polite, uneven applause. Around me, people were glancing at each other, mouthing questions to each other. One man shrugged and shook his head, too puzzled to answer his friend's question. A woman near me whispered to her companion, "Is he reciting from the auction house's website, or what?"

Her friend said, "Hardly the heavy hitting thinker I thought he was."

"Maybe there's more..."

But there wasn't. Knox urged anyone with questions to come see him privately, then said "thank you." He walked off stage, stepping onto the lawn and striding away with his usual haughty confidence. All around him, though, people were staring at him, whispering, even smiling with condescension. Had his little speech damaged his reputation as top dog?

"What was that about?" I asked Teddy.

"Maybe Knox Kensington is losing it. Or maybe he has a hidden agenda."

"If he does, I'd love to know what it is."

Teddy grinned. "I'm going to ask him."

He explained what his plan was, and I reluctantly agreed to play along. It seemed exactly like the kind of plan Teddy would've concocted when we were kids.

He found Knox by the coffee station and cornered him, pestering him for an interview until the tall man gave in. Maybe hoping to get rid of Teddy for good.

They wandered toward a bench under a sycamore tree. Which was what Teddy had told me he would arrange. I was standing behind the sycamore tree, well within earshot of their conversation.

Teddy began by praising Knox for his speech.

"It was necessary," Knox said.

"An interesting choice of words," Teddy said.

"As I said on stage, at Bishop & Company, we take our responsibility to the artwork and the artist seriously. We want to shine a light on art. We don't want it to disappear into obscurity."

"You mean art may disappear because the public loses interest?"

"That's one interpretation."

"Or because someone steals the artwork?"

Silence. I couldn't see them. But I imagined Knox nodding.

Teddy said, "Like Joe Rudder tried to steal a Julia Larke painting?"

Again, silence from Knox.

But Teddy persisted. "Joe Rudder used to work for Bishop & Company, didn't he?"

"That was long ago," Knox said.

"But you knew him. Were you friends?"

"Who could be friends with that man?"

"Did you know he was in town?"

Again, silence. But Teddy, maybe knowing I couldn't see a head nod, said, "So you did know. You saw him. Did you know he was here to steal a Larke painting?"

"I didn't know anything," Knox snapped. "And I'm not here to discuss Joe Rudder. I'm here to discuss Julia Larke and her art."

After that, he refused to be led back to the topic. Teddy made a few attempts, then gave up, and they talked about Julia Larke and her legacy. Knox grudgingly admitted Larke was a major rediscovery. He even acknowledged that Larke House had done "a fine job" curating Larke's art and bringing her importance to light.

Then Knox broke off the interview and the soft tread of his shoes on the grass receded. He was gone. Teddy told me the coast was clear and I came out from behind the tree, taking Knox's place on the bench.

"There you have it," Teddy said. "Knox knew Joe Rudder—and knew him well enough to recognize him."

"Which means that..."

"Well, how about this: Knox's impromptu talk on stage was an argument against allowing private buyers to take artwork out of the public sphere. So maybe he knew Joe Rudder intended to steal a Larke painting and sell it on the black market."

I frowned. "But the painting the killer stole isn't worth a lot. At best a couple of thousand dollars. Why would Knox

Kensington spend so much energy on this minor work by Larke?"

"Maybe he believes all artwork deserves to be protected. Even enough to kill someone."

"Well, I don't know about that..."

I considered the situation. Joe Rudder had been willing to lie and sneak around to get his hands on a painting. Mom's presence made him nervous. But that didn't scare him off. Maybe because he knew he was close to something valuable.

I said, "Teddy, what if Joe Rudder was looking for a much more valuable painting?"

"What do you mean?"

"Well, the two sisters were found by someone in Boston. They were hidden behind other works of art. Maybe Joe Rudder knew where the third sister was."

"I guess..." Teddy wrinkled his nose.

"You're not convinced?"

"The other two sisters were found in Boston. Don't you think that's where the third will turn up? Why would one be lying around at the Lakeview Inn?"

He had a point. Whoever had found the paintings in Boston might discover the third sister. Maybe they already had, and Bishop & Company would announced it any day now.

Teddy said, "What if the painting Joe was trying to steal —the one the killer took—was worth more than we think?"

"An undiscovered Larke? A new masterpiece?"

Teddy nodded. "And I know of only three people who could identify such a painting."

"Miranda, Esther, and Knox."

He was right. Everything came back to those three.

21

The symposium was over and the crowd flowed down Chestnut Hill toward the town docks. Once again, Miranda had booked the Breeze for dinner and drinks, and the guests, following her, were chatting on their way down the street.

The mood had turned light-hearted. A man made a joke about Manet being mistaken for Monet and his companions laughed. A woman said, "Have I told you this one? So Picasso, Van Gogh, and Jackson Pollack walk into a bar..."

Teddy was talking to Esther, trying to repeat what he'd done with Knox—wheedling information out of her while I listened. I trailed behind them.

As we crossed Main Street, a figure broke off from the crowd, hurrying down the sidewalk.

I stopped. There was no mistaking that tall man. It was Knox Kensington, and he was heading in the wrong direction. Alone.

I gave him a head start, falling back from Teddy and Esther. And then further back—until I was the only person on the sidewalk. The last of the symposium guests disappeared around the corner, heading to the town docks.

Then I followed Knox.

He strode down the street, over the bridge, and then crossed the street to the Lakeview Inn. His long legs could carry him far and fast. In fact, he seemed on the cusp of running. He bolted up the front steps and disappeared inside.

In the reception, I looked around. Empty seating area. Abandoned reception desk. Silence. He was gone.

Aunt Lil popped up from behind the reception counter, like a rustling, billowy jack in the box, and I jumped.

"Don't you have a symposium dinner at the Breeze?" she asked.

I leaned close to her and dropped my voice. "I'm looking for Knox Kensington."

"He's in his room," she whispered, clearly enjoying the conspiratorial whispering, "packing."

"I knew it," I said. "I knew he was up to something."

"He asked me to order a taxi for the airport," Aunt Lil said. "I suggested that once he came down, he could wait in the lounge." A mischievous smile spread across her face. "Maybe the Fates will conspire to delay the cab…"

That would give me time to talk to him. I headed for the lounge.

Above the mantelpiece, the empty space where Julia Larke's painting had hung looked so desolate now. Joe Rudder had found the real deal: an original Julia Larke. But the killer had swapped it for an imitation. So where was the original? Long gone, probably. But then how had the killer managed to smuggle the painting out of the inn without being seen?

I glanced around the room, and the armchair caught my

attention. What had Aunt Lil said about her blanket vanishing? A blanket could come in handy for a thief. I pictured a figure with a canvas wrapped in a blanket hurrying out of the inn.

Then shook my head.

Blanket or not, you'd attract attention by sneaking around town with a big canvas under your arm. It seemed more likely that the killer had returned to the porch, hiding among the crowd. And not with a painting under the arm. But then where was it?

The door to the lounge opened and Knox walked in, rolling a suitcase alongside him. He saw me and stopped. I stared at his suitcase. It was small, small enough for the overhead compartment. But wasn't that too small for a canvas?

"Where are you hurrying off to?" I asked.

"I'm not hurrying," he grumbled. "Even if I wanted to stay, I have business in Boston to attend to. Urgent business."

"Now that Joe Rudder's gone..."

"What are you implying?"

"You knew Joe."

"I knew *of* Joe. Joe Rudder worked briefly at Bishop & Company years before I joined. I don't appreciate the insinuations you're making..."

"Why did you really come to Allington, Mr. Kensington?"

"I came because Julia Larke has made Bishop & Company a lot of money. Theodore Pullman, the client who's selling the two sisters, has entrusted us with a big responsibility..."

"And an interest in finding more Larke paintings—at whatever the cost?"

"That's enough. If you want to sling mud, you can talk to my lawyer. I'm not having some Podunk muckraker slander me. Goodbye."

He turned on his heels, yanked open the door to the hallway, and disappeared from view. In that instant, the door at the opposite end of the lounge opened and Aunt Lil peeked her head in—"Mr. Kensington? Your taxi's here..."—and the breeze blew through the lounge. The draft grabbed the door Knox had walked through and heaved it shut with a hefty bang. The cold draft blew past me and something rattled behind me.

Aunt Lil said, "Where did Knox go?"

I waved her over. "I felt something..."

"Don't tell me you have feelings for Knox Kensington."

"Seriously, the draft. It made something rattle back here."

I approached the fireplace, put a hand on the mantle, and peered into the ashy chamber.

"Is the chimney open?"

"No," Aunt Lil said. "I only keep it open in winter." She checked. "See? It's closed."

"Then what's causing the draft? Because there's definitely a draft coming through the fireplace."

I crouched down. The ashes seemed to have been moved, pushed into heaps to either side.

I pointed that out to Aunt Lil.

She said, "I didn't do that."

"And look at those scuff marks on the back wall."

She leaned into the fireplace. "Looks like someone's scraped the metal plate at the back. Maybe with a poker. Now, why would someone do that?"

"Only one way to find out."

I grabbed an iron poker and stuck the sharp end into the

gap between the metal plate at the back of the fireplace and the stone wall. As I levered the poker, there was a loud groan and then a crack.

The metal plate swung outward.

I gaped at the opening. Then said, "It's a door."

I threw the poker aside and pulled open the door, revealing a compartment within. Stone walls on three sides. Broken bricks and debris. And a hole in the back wall through which the wind whistled.

"That looks like a tunnel," Aunt Lil said, peering inside. "But it's collapsed."

It didn't matter. My attention was on the object leaning against one of the walls. It was covered by a blanket.

"Look," I said.

"My blanket," Aunt Lil exclaimed. "That dirty rat."

She pulled the blanket off the object it covered, revealing a canvas.

It was the Julia Larke painting she'd found in the attic. The one Joe Rudder must've been trying to steal. Up in the right-hand corner, the bird hovered in the sky.

I reached in and carefully removed it from the dusty compartment. At least the thief had the decency to protect the artwork with a blanket. I set the canvas down and examined it for any signs of damage.

"Hold on," I said. "What's this?"

On the back side, something sat within the wooden frame. The object, filling out the natural cavity formed by the supports, fit perfectly. Small nails driven into the wood held it in place.

"I didn't notice this before," Aunt Lil said. "Not even when I was hanging the painting. What is it?"

I bent the nails. Rust had eaten them and two snapped off in my hands. Finally, I pulled the object out of the frame.

"Another canvas," I said.

Then I turned it around, so we could see the painting itself.

I gasped. Butterflies fluttered crazily in my stomach.

"Is this what I think it is?" Aunt Lil whispered, awe in her voice.

"It is," I whispered, just as awestruck. "It's Julia Larke's third sister."

22

Deputy Douglas guarded the entrance to the lounge. The door was open, and he glanced into the hallway every second, as if he expected someone to appear. A door slammed somewhere. He jumped and reached for his gun. Then, when the jangling of Aunt Lil's bangles passed down the corridor outside, he relaxed and let his hands fall to his side again.

"Poor Doug," I told Mom.

Mom, keeping her voice low, said, "He's afraid a bunch of art terrorists will burst through the door."

"At least Miranda's happy."

Miranda, who was examining the painting for the umpteenth time, heard me and turned. Her whole face lit up with joy. She'd been chattering nonstop about the painting since she saw it. She'd urged us to admire the minute brush strokes in the hair and the rippling quality to the light. Not to mention the way the woman reclined—powerful yet relaxed—which gave the scene an understated drama.

"A matriarch in her natural condition," Miranda said, beaming at the third sister. "A woman proud of her body."

I laughed. "Sounds like you're already writing your first essay on the subject."

"You don't understand. This is huge. Huge. We've found all three sisters now—the triptych is reunited: the oldest sister in the middle, reclining, with her younger sisters in armchairs, framing her. The masterpiece is complete."

"I understand we're looking at a painting that's worth half a million dollars," I said

Mom nodded. "That's an amount people will kill for."

Miranda's smile died and her face fell. "Awful, isn't it? That someone would want to kill a man. Joe Rudder must've worked out that the painting was hidden here at the inn..."

"Pullman House," I said, my heart doing a little backflip. "Of course."

"Of course, what?" Mom asked.

"The person selling the two sisters through Bishop & Company—his name is Pullman. It must be a descendant of the Pullmans who owned this house. I bet they took two of the paintings with them but, for whatever reason, not the third. Probably because the Pullmans didn't realize what was hidden behind the Larke imitations. Now, living in Boston, they discovered the secret but didn't realize there was a third painting still hidden in the old mansion that the family sold years ago."

"But Joe made the connection," Miranda said.

"Clever Joe," Mom said. "In fact, it sounds uncharacteristically clever, considering what we know about Joe Rudder."

I scratched my eyebrow. She was right. Joe's focus was on small-time discoveries, tricking people out of antiques that might be worth hundreds of dollars more than they realized. But not hundreds of thousands. But if he had help....

"What if it wasn't Joe who figured it out?" I suggested. "Maybe someone else did, and Joe was sent to get it. So who would be clever enough—?"

"Knox Kensington," Miranda said.

I glanced over at the fireplace, where I'd stood when Know came in before his departure. Had he hoped to be alone, so he could retrieve the painting? But no, it was Aunt Lil who'd suggested he wait in the lounge, and besides...

"If it was Knox," I said, "why send Joe to steal the painting and then kill him?"

Miranda shrugged and again leaned close to the painting to study it.

Mom said, "Unless both Joe and Knox knew, and Knox wanted to beat Joe to it."

"That's possible," I agreed. "Joe uses Miranda's speech as a distraction to grab the painting, and Knox realizes what he's up to. He knocks Joe down with the bust. But the alarm alerts others. So he hides the painting, substituting it for the copy that Joe himself planned to swap it with. Then runs out of the room and sneaks back into the crowd. But he fails to retrieve the painting hidden in the fireplace, because there are too many people around the inn. And now, with his plans ruined, he runs."

Mom frowned. "But why run now—without the painting?"

"Yeah, that doesn't make sense..."

"I'll bet he's not as far away as we're supposed to believe."

Miranda patted the canvas frame. "All the more reason for this painting to be put in a safe place." She turned to Mom. "Don't you agree, Chief Lee?"

Mom was gazing at the painting, her head cocked. As if studying it. "You're right—it needs to be kept in a safe place," she said. "Which is why I'm taking the painting home."

"To Larke House," Miranda said.

But Mom shook her head. "To Broadstairs House."

23

"Just talked to the state police," Mom said, coming into the living room from the back porch of Broadstairs House, and pocketing her cell phone. "They tracked down Knox Kensington's flight back to Boston. Guess what?"

"He never boarded his plane?"

Mom smiled. "Bingo."

Mom's idea to move the painting to our home still puzzled me. She'd sent Dad, Joy, and Scottie over to Ray and Roxie's house to keep any "civilians" out of her plan.

Unfortunately, they'd taken Dad's lasagna with them.

But Aunt Lil had insisted on joining us. She was in the kitchen making a roasted broccoli and sweet potato quinoa salad that she said would counterbalance the planetary alignments.

"And how does Knox Kensington's whereabouts fit with your plan?" I asked.

"Whoever wants that painting will turn up," Mom said. "They'll think our home is unguarded. The best place to grab the painting before it gets put in a vault somewhere."

I nodded. "So, if Knox killed Joe, he'll make an appearance tonight?"

Why didn't I feel more confident in this plan? Maybe because something about the whole murder and art theft still wasn't adding up. A piece of the puzzle was still missing...

The phone rang. The landline. Mom gave me a significant look, a raised eyebrow, as if the games were about to begin.

She picked up the phone. "Lee residence, Charlene speaking. Oh, hi, Miranda." She listened. "Yes, the painting is perfectly fine. Where exactly is it? I can't divulge that kind of information. Only that it's safe."

Mom and I stood in the living room. She glanced over at the painting. The third piece of Julia Larke's masterpiece, the oldest sister, leaned against the wall on top of a low bookshelf. Next to it stood a framed photograph of Dad on the dock with his fishing rod. A big grin on his face as he held up a fish.

Mom said, "Miranda, I assure you. It's perfectly safe. No need to come check. We'll talk in the morning."

She hung up.

"Quinoa salad's ready," Aunt Lil crooned from the kitchen.

"I could be eating lasagna," I told Mom. "You owe me."

She smiled. "If this works out, we'll eat lasagna every night for a month."

As we moved toward the kitchen, my gaze fell on a nearby window to the porch. In the dark outside, a shadow shifted. Then I saw the stars in the sky beyond. I heard the scuff of a shoe. Somehow had been standing there.

I dropped my voice. "Mom, someone's outside."

Mom touched her gun, but left it in the holster. "Knox?"

"I didn't see..."

She put a finger to her lips. Then whispered, "I hear someone..."

She moved to the front door without making a sound. Positioned her back to the wall so she could open the door with her left hand. And still reach her gun with her right.

She motioned for me to stand back.

Then she unholstered her gun and pulled open the door.

Outside, Teddy was standing inches from my mom, his hand raised in a fist. About to knock. His mouth formed a silent, surprised O.

He recovered. "I was about to knock," he whispered, glancing over his shoulder, then back at Mom. "I was coming to visit Parker when I saw Esther Winch snooping around your house. Peering in windows. I thought I'd better alert you."

"Thanks, Teddy," Mom said.

"I'm right here," I said from behind her.

Teddy stepped inside, a look of relief on his face, and my mom moved aside. He said, "I've been looking all over for you, Park. I got to the Breeze and you'd disappeared. Vanished without a trace. I was beginning to worry..."

Then he saw it. The painting. And his eyes widened.

"Holy moly," he said. "Is that—?"

"The third sister," Esther said from the doorway.

"Good grief," Mom said, and I knew what she was thinking: if one more person showed up, her whole plan to flush out the killer-thief would fall apart.

Just then the beams from a pair of headlights swept through the open door as a car pulled into our driveway. It came to a sudden halt. Miranda got out, and standing with the door open, gazed up at the house.

Esther, glancing back at Miranda, tried to force her way through the door, but Mom blocked her.

Aunt Lil came out of the kitchen, wiping her hands on a dish towel. "Oh, we've got visitors. Wonderful. The more, the merrier."

Mom said, "They're not staying for dinner, Lil. Are you, Ms. Winch?"

Esther frowned, and—tight-lipped—tried to see past her to where the painting stood. "I'm here to talk to Lil about her painting."

"My painting?" Aunt Lil asked, surprised.

"You found the third sister at the inn. You bought Pullman House and everything within it. So the painting is legally yours."

"That may be true," Aunt Lil said. "But so what?"

"So I want to buy it."

Aunt Lil stared at her. "You want to buy the Larke?"

"That's what I said, isn't it? I'll give you a fair price."

"But I'm not selling."

Esther looked taken aback. "You're not..." Then she scowled, and threw another glance over her shoulder. "Miranda. She got to you first, didn't she? That weasel."

"Miranda didn't get to me. Nobody did. In fact, you're the first person to offer me money." Aunt Lil smiled. "It's very flattering. But the answer is still no."

"You don't even know how much I'm willing to offer."

"No, but I imagine it's a lot."

I said, "That's right. Knox Kensington could probably get you half a million for the painting."

"Knox," Esther said through gritted teeth, "Kensington. Don't talk to me about Knox Kensington."

"What about Knox Kensington?" Miranda said, coming up behind Esther.

"Stay out of this, Miranda."

Mom pushed Esther out the door. "Why don't you two talk it over outside..."

Esther hissed, "I'll be back. I'm not letting Larke House snap this one up."

"Chief Lee," Miranda said. "I really insist—"

Mom shut the door on the two of them. Their bickering didn't stop, though—I could hear their raised voices as they moved away from the house.

I said, "Amazing. I get the feeling Esther doesn't care about the painting as much as she cares about making life hard for Miranda."

"Academic rivals," Teddy said, shaking his head. But he kept looking at the third sister with big eyes. He said, "You're sure this one is real? This is the real deal?"

"Positive," I said, earning a hard look from Mom.

Mom said, "The exhibition is over for the evening, Teddy. You can visit Parker tomorrow."

She showed him the door.

"I could stay and help," he said, as she put a hand on his back and pushed him out.

"You'd be a big help," Mom said, "if you left."

I grimaced. Sometimes Mom had the social graces of a wolf.

She shut the door, leaned her back against it, and let out a long breath.

"So much for that plan."

The three of us—Mom, Aunt Lil, and I—returned to the painting. Amazing how much trouble one canvas could cause.

"Tomorrow," Mom said, "we move the painting to a safer place. To a vault."

That night, after our surprisingly delicious quinoa salad

dinner—and after Aunt Lil left—Mom posted Deputy Douglas outside our home. I made up the couch with sheets from the closet, so I could sleep close to the painting. After brushing my teeth and washing my face in the bathroom upstairs, I returned to the living room. I was surprised to see Mom in her pajamas. She was putting sheets on the second couch.

"What are you doing up?" I asked.

"If you're sleeping down here," she said, "then so am I. And we might as well make the best of the situation." She smiled. "So, wanna watch a movie?"

I grinned. "Do you even have to ask?"

We made cups of chamomile tea, curled up next to each other on the couch, and rewatched "The Lake House" for the umpteenth time. I leaned against her. If I'd been in the big city, this cozy moment wouldn't have happened. Another point for Allington.

24

The doors to Larke House swung open and Miranda stepped out. She spread open her arms and smiled.

"Welcome back home."

She was talking to the painting, of course, which Deputy Douglas carried up the steps. His hands shook a little and a bead of sweat trickled down his face. Poor Deputy Douglas.

As he handed Miranda the painting of the third sister, he gave her a tight nod. Then wiped the sweat from his face.

Miranda carried the painting inside. Her shoes clicked on the marble floors.

"We made it," Deputy Douglas said, sounding relieved.

"The painting's not safe yet," Mom said.

In the massive entrance hall to Larke House, Deputy Douglas positioned himself by the door. He put a hand on his holster. Mom peered off into every nook and cranny, as if thieves might be hiding there, likely to leap out at any moment. In the gargantuan oil painting on the wall, Mr. Larke scowled down at us.

"Don't worry," Miranda said over her shoulder as she

crossed the marble floor toward a doorway at the back. "I have the safest place in Allington right here in Larke House. Follow me."

Carrying the precious painting, she led us down a corridor. A kitchen opened up to the left, but she turned right, stepping through a doorway where the door stood open. Down a staircase.

"Watch your head."

The lintel was low and Mom had to duck to clear it. I took more after my dad, but even so, I was careful not to bump my head.

We headed down the steps and into a cellar. A long room with a vaulted ceiling contained rows and rows of wine bottles.

"Mr. Larke was a wine collector," Miranda explained, "and part of his will decreed that the Larke House Estate must continue to manage his collection."

"So you're a wine expert, too?" I asked.

Miranda chuckled. "Wouldn't that be something. No, I outsource that task to our local wine store."

She turned down another corridor, which took us past more storage rooms. Some with furniture, others with neatly stacked boxes.

The arches that seemed to support the ceiling sweated. The air was damp and cool. It felt as if we were far underground, deep into the bedrock.

The corridor ended in a massive stone wall. Set into the wall was a huge vault, like something you'd see in a bank.

"This wall was carved straight out of the rock under Chestnut Hill," Miranda explained.

The vault, in contrast to the surroundings, was relatively modern. A sticker near the safe's keypad said, "Inspected by

K's Lock & Key," and someone had written a recent date in pen below it.

"See?" Miranda said. "It was inspected recently. You'd need dynamite to break into this thing. And only I can open it."

Ignoring the keypad, she pressed her finger onto a biometric fingerprint scanner. Something clicked within the safe. She swung open the door. Inside were rows of shelves with boxes. No other paintings, though.

"Do you store art down here?"

"Not usually," she said. "It isn't suitable for long-term storage. Too damp. But the third sister will be fine for a few days while we arrange for her new home."

She placed the painting on a shelf, smiling as she admired it again. She stepped forward to brush dust off its frame. Then stepped back again. I had the feeling she could stay down here in the vault all day, goggling at the masterpiece.

But finally, we all backed out of the vault and Miranda shut the massive door. It slid into place with a hefty thump. She pressed her finger on the scanner again. I listened closely for the snick of the lock, and got instead a *snick-snick-THUNK*. Not just one bolt, but many.

Miranda was right. What thief could possibly break into this vault?

$$25$$

The next morning, Sunday, clouds covered the sky and mist rolled across Lake Allington. Despite the damp chill to the air, Mom and I sat on the inn's back porch. Across from us sat Scottie and Miranda. Aunt Lil had served us all cups of warm tea—a strong Assam with a malty, toasty taste—and then left us alone to help Scottie and Miranda reach a truce.

"Larke House draws a lot of visitors," Scottie was saying, "and you're telling me I can't sell to all those tourists. That's totally unfair. No way I'm agreeing to that."

"Unbelievable," Miranda said, throwing up her hands. "How'd you like it if I hung around your ice-cream shop and sold my own homemade gelato to tourists?"

"You're comparing apples and oranges."

"Am I? Or do you feel you have a right to sell your wares anywhere in Allington?"

"Well..." Scottie shrugged. "I wouldn't say *anywhere*."

Mom said, "It's a fair question, Scottie. With that cargo bike of yours, you can roam all over town. Where do you see the boundaries for your business?"

"I guess you said it, Mom. Where my cargo bike can go."

"So, if you printed books, would you go to Peony Lane to sell them?"

He chuckled. "I don't think Balthazar at Balthazar Books would be happy about that."

Miranda broke in. "How is that different from Larke House?"

"It's completely different," Scottie said, turning serious. "Look, if I started selling copies of Stephen King novels, then Balthazar Books would be right to go after me."

"So would Stephen King and his publisher," I said.

"Just an example," Scottie shot back at me. Then he turned back to Mom. "But Julia Larke is Allington, and Allington is Julia Larke. It would be like telling people they couldn't sell Thoreau t-shirts at Walden Pond. Or Hemingway mugs at Finca La Vigia..."

"Uh, Scottie," I said. "I don't think just anyone's allowed to set up a souvenir stand by Walden Pond. And I don't know how the Cuban authorities would feel about hawkers at Hemingway House."

"I'm making analogies," Scottie said. "It's the principle that matters."

"I can't believe you're talking about principles," Miranda said.

"Oh, and why not? Who gave you a monopoly on principles?"

"I don't have a monopoly on principles—"

"You sure have a monopoly on Julia Larke. I have a right to her as much as you do. As much as anyone does." Scottie's voice rose and color bloomed on his cheeks. "Julia celebrates Allington in her paintings. She could've left for New York or Paris, but she didn't. She didn't abandon us. She stayed in Allington, because she loved this town as much as

I do. Yeah, I love this town, I love Julia Larke, and I don't think it's fair that you keep her to yourself."

His eyes glistened. He quickly turned away and wiped a hand across his eyes. Miranda and I gaped at each other. I looked at Mom. This wasn't like Scottie. But she seemed completely unconcerned by her son's show of emotion. Maybe she was used to Scottie veering from indignant to emotional, having seen him melt down as a kid when he didn't get the Christmas presents he wanted.

Mom steepled her hands and said, "Good. We've reached the heart of the matter. You both love Julia Larke. You both love Allington. That's a beautiful thing. And importantly, it's common ground."

Scottie crossed his arms on his chest. "Common ground," he snorted and shook his head.

"But the way you've been expressing that love," Mom said, ignoring him. "Well, we know where that's landed us. So let's think about another way to do it. Let's think—"

With a loud jangling of bracelets and necklaces, Aunt Lil burst through the door from the inside, clearly excited. "We have a visitor."

Knox Kensington, following her, stepped out onto the porch.

He glared at us. Then zeroed in on Miranda. "Miranda, you fool. How could you let that painting out of your sight for even a second?"

26

"That painting isn't safe," Knox insisted.

"If you saw the vault we put it in…" I said.

But he dismissed me with the wave of a hand.

Aunt Lil said, "Sit down, Knox, and have a cup of tea."

He gazed at us, his lip curled. Somehow he overcame his distaste and joined us at the table. Lil brought two more cups—one of them for herself—poured tea, and sat down.

Everyone was looking at Knox. He looked harried, with signs of fatigue on his face. He sipped his tea. Then said, "I knew Joe Rudder."

"News flash," I said. Then, knowing he wouldn't respond well to snarky comments, I added, "From when he worked at Bishop & Company?"

Knox shook his head. "That was before I joined the auction house. But people told me about him. He was using his position to acquire antiques and sell them on the black market. When that was discovered, he was told to leave. And yet the man had no shame. He would turn up at events and auctions, hobnobbing with old colleagues as if we were all pals."

"Nobody said anything?"

"People at Bishop & Company are too polite. Our boss is spineless." He grimaced. "And Joe wasn't a complete idiot. He knew that we couldn't legally bar him from public events. After all, he'd been quietly dismissed. No charges were ever brought against him, so we couldn't simply call the police."

Mom nodded. "We can't do much based on hearsay."

"That's right," Knox said. "So when I heard that Joe was heading to Allington—" He stopped himself and looked around the table. "One moment. Let's back up. Do you know who Arthur X is?"

Of course we all knew who Arthur X was—he was all over the news and social media.

I said, "We found his book, *This Art Belongs to Art*, among Joe's things."

"That wasn't a coincidence," Knox said. "When the Pullmans discovered the two sisters, Arthur X became obsessed with buying them. But he has a history of unscrupulous behavior, not least in how he handles art. He refuses to lend to museums. He has a harebrained idea of putting all his art on the moon. He's even destroyed invaluable art, because he disagreed with it."

I'd read about that, of course. A feminist artist had denounced his vocal sexism. That offended him. So he'd bought one of her works of art, poured a 2,000-dollar bottle of absinthe over it, and set it on fire.

Knox said, "Bishop & Company has blacklisted Arthur X. We won't allow him to buy at auction—whether directly or through a handler. We're encouraging other auction houses to blacklist him, too."

I said, "I didn't realize—"

"That we have morals?" He raised an eyebrow. "Young lady, we may be a for-profit firm, but we're first and foremost committed to art. Arthur X is only committed to himself."

Knox wasn't who I'd made him out to be. Sure he was a stuffy, snooty snob with a dash of male chauvinism. But he nevertheless had some principles—and he was willing to fight for them.

I said, "So, let me guess, Arthur X blew up when he learned the Pullmans were selling through Bishop & Company."

"That's right, and he vowed to get his hands on the third sister. In fact, he was the one who tracked down the most likely location of the missing painting."

"And then he sent Joe."

Knox frowned. "Not just Joe. He sent out word to his network of scavengers. In the end, he hired three people, promising the one who got the painting a huge finder's fee. Arthur X likes that kind of thing. He calls it "healthy competition." Well, one of those rival scavengers is a friend of mine. He pretended to be open to Arthur X's plans when, in fact, he dislikes the man as much as I do. He could tell me about Arthur X's plans but, unfortunately, not who the other two scavengers were. My friend chose to stay away from Allington, but I cleared my calendar and headed straight for the symposium."

"And when you saw Joe Rudder—"

"When I saw him, I knew he was one of the two scavengers. I knew there'd be trouble."

Mom frowned. "You should've informed me."

"Local cops often bungle these sensitive matters," Knox said with a shrug. "I did what I had to do."

Mom showed no immediate reaction. Or at least her face

didn't. But her hands, which rested on the table, clenched into fists, her knuckles whitening.

I sighed. Yes, Knox was still a snooty jerk. But he seemed to be telling the truth. All along he'd wanted to stop Joe— and whoever the third scavenger was. But that didn't mean killing anyone. And it certainly didn't make sense that after discovering the third sister, he'd hide it in the fireplace.

I glanced at Miranda. She was staring at Knox, nodding. She too would've been motivated to stop Joe. But hide the painting in the fireplace? No way.

I said, "So the killer is most likely the third scavenger."

"A rival of Joe's," Miranda said.

Knox nodded. "Which is why I worry the painting isn't safe."

"It's in my vault," Miranda said. "And nothing and nobody can—"

Her phone rang. She pulled it out of her pocket and frowned at the screen. Then answered. "Yes? Yes, that's me. Oh, right, the password is—"

She cupped her hands over the phone and muttered something I couldn't hear. Then she listened. And as she listened, her face drained of color.

"A break-in? But—but—how's that possible?"

27

"This way," Miranda said.

She jogged down the stairs to the cellar. Behind her, Knox, with his long legs, kept up the pace. Mom and I made up the rearguard. After running to the cars, driving across town, and then bolting up the steps to Larke House, the cold, damp air hit me hard. I shivered.

What would we find? A failed burglary attempt? It had to be. No one could get into that massive vault.

When the burglary alarm went off, the security company had deployed a guard to Larke House. She'd discovered an open patio door leading to the garden, the lock apparently picked. Once the thief had stepped inside the house, though, the sensors caught the movement and set off the remote alarms. Cameras had caught the masked burglar leaving again, carrying a large object. Now the guard and Deputy Douglas were checking the entire mansion, just in case there was a second burglar.

"One thing is breaking into the mansion," Miranda said. We hurried past the racks of wine bottles and turned into the big corridor with the vault. "Another thing is—"

She stopped. Knox cursed.

Up ahead the door to the vault stood wide open.

Miranda ran into the vault. Knox followed her.

Miranda spun around herself, eyes wide. "No, no, no..."

But it was true. The painting was gone. Mom and I entered the vault, and I spun around, looking at the shelves. The place where Miranda so lovingly had placed the third sister yesterday was empty.

"I told you," Knox said.

Miranda buried her face in her hands.

"How could this happen?" she said. "No one can open that safe but me. No one."

I said, "What about your staff?"

"Larke House staff are all volunteers—or they're hired for events—and I don't give them access to the vault."

"The security company, then?"

Miranda shook her head. "The vault isn't their responsibility."

Mom said, "Makes sense. And if someone from security was involved, they would've disabled the alarm before breaking in. But then who...?"

I stepped out of the vault and studied the giant door. No signs of forced entry. Literally only dynamite—if even that—would be able to force this slab or iron open. And only Miranda's fingerprint could open the biometric lock.

"Miranda," I said. "If only you can open the vault, then what happens if—well, you can't—say, if you die?"

Miranda gave me a sharp look. "If I die? What are you suggesting?"

"Please, I need to know—what would happen? Is there a code for that keypad?"

"No, only my finger can open the vault. I've never

programmed the keypad to accept a passcode. But in case of an emergency..."

Before she could finish her sentence, I knew. The realization hit me hard—my head spun, and I grabbed hold of the door to steady myself.

Oh, no...

I pulled back the huge metal door and studied the keypad, with its biometric scanner and the slot for an override key. Then looked at the sticker on the outside.

It said, "K's Lock & Key."

I was right, then.

"I know who our thief is," I said, and everyone turned to me.

28

On the Lakeview Inn's back porch, I gazed out at the view of the lake and the woods beyond. The view that Julia Larke herself had studied and painted so many times. Aunt Lil leaned against the railing next to me. We were alone. After I'd explained things, Mom had alerted the state police and then sped off with Deputy Douglas. Miranda and Knox had gone off to look, too. Aunt Lil and I had called everyone we knew in town, so they could keep their eyes open for the thief. Thief and killer.

"I'm such a fool, Aunt Lil. All this time I thought Teddy Kendall was my friend, and he was using me to get close to the painting."

"You acted in good faith," Aunt Lil said. "Besides, Mercury is retrograde, and when that happens, even the best of minds may be clouded."

"I should've known," I said, ignoring her reassuring words. "He must've tried to get into the lounge a dozen times. The morning after the murder, he showed up late to the symposium. I bet he was sneaking around the inn. But he couldn't get into the lounge undisturbed to retrieve the painting. And then we found the hiding place and moved the painting to Broadstairs House."

"And then he showed up that night."

I nodded. "When we caught Teddy snooping around outside, he got lucky. Esther turned up, and that made her look like the suspicious person. When really she was completely honest about why she came: she wanted to buy the painting."

I shook my head.

"K's Lock & Key. Why didn't I realize the danger beforehand?"

"Because you trusted Teddy, of course," Aunt Lil said. "How could you know his parents installed Miranda's safe, and therefore have an override key?"

I said, "Teddy worked at K's Lock & Key. He would've known how to get hold of override keys. When we brought the painting to Larke House, we played right into his hands. Ironically, the painting *was* safer at Broadstairs House." Imagining Teddy's reaction, I grimaced. "He must've been doing a happy dance. What an idiot I was to trust him..."

Aunt Lil put an arm around my shoulders. "What's worse—trusting an old friend or treating him with suspicion? Trust is a beautiful thing. Without it, we wouldn't be whole human beings. The blame here is not on you. It's on him. And that awful man, Arthur X." Then she added, "Those dirty rats."

I smiled. Oh, Lil—she could cheer me up at even the worst of moments.

"I guess me wallowing in self-pity won't help us catch Teddy. We've got to find him before he gets to Arthur X with that painting."

"But your mom and the state police—not to mention

most of Allington—has been looking." Aunt Lil shook her head. "Teddy seems to have vanished."

"I know. But I've got a feeling he's close..."

The truth lay, as Dad always said, in the basic facts. Where would we find Teddy? When we were kids, he gravitated toward places away from his unhappy home. Pullman House, in particular. Which was why he knew all the inn's hiding places. But we'd searched the inn, and he was nowhere in sight.

I peered out over the lake. Above the far shore of the lake, an aircraft rose above the Allington Woods. A helicopter heading across the lake. Heading toward Gull Island.

My chest tightened. Of course.

"I know where he is."

29

Thanks to my rowing skills—and a big dose of desperation—I reached Gull Island before the helicopter. But the distant buzzing rose to a roar as it drew closer. I hurried across the island. The brambles tore at me. I pushed thorny branches aside, crashing through bushes. So what if Teddy heard me coming? Getting to him fast was what mattered.

Aunt Lil had offered to come, but after failing to reach my mom, I'd asked her to stay at the inn and keep trying— get as much help as possible.

As I got closer to the clearing, I heard a droning sound. The helicopter, I thought at first, but then realized there was something else, too. The drone of an engine—different from the helicopter—coming across the water.

I gazed through the trees. A flash of blue across the water. A boat on the lake, speeding around the island.

I grinned. "Mom."

The police speedboat curved around the island, disappearing from view.

No time to waste. I rushed into the clearing with the

cabin. The rickety front door was shut. I grabbed the handle. But yanking only shook the door in the frame.

"Bolted," I muttered to myself.

Teddy must've fixed the door, knowing we'd come looking for him. In a minute or two, Arthur X—or more likely, one of his associates—would arrive by helicopter. How could I stop Teddy? How could I save Larke's painting?

"Teddy, open up!"

From inside, Teddy shouted, "Get out of here, Park. Go away."

"I'm not leaving without that painting."

A clatter from within. Then a heavy thump. The walls of the old cabin shook.

I stepped back from the cabin. Then threw myself at the door, slamming into it. Pain flared in my shoulder. The hinges cried out and ripped free, the old wood frame splintering. The door fell with a crash, and I tumbled inside.

I fell to my knees. The cabin was empty, except for the usual detritus. The thump I heard must've been the trapdoor shutting. Teddy was on the roof.

Right by my hands lay the snake-like rope that had startled me when I found Scottie. Snake Island was what Teddy used to call this place. But as my fact-checking mom would no doubt say, *There are no snakes on Gull Island.*

I hesitated, still on my hands and knees. Then grabbed the rope and got to my feet.

I threw myself against the flimsy trapdoor, breaking it open. I climbed up the stairs, emerging onto the open-air floor above.

The trees on the island shook, as if a sudden storm had blown in, and the wind whipped against me. The rotor roar of the helicopter was everywhere. As if I were inside the sound.

Teddy stood near the edge of the cabin, looking up. He hugged the cloth-covered canvas to his chest.

I took a step toward him. "Come on, Teddy. Let it go. It's over."

"It's only over when I give this to its new owner."

"Arthur X? You think we're going to let him land here?"

Then the helicopter reared up over the island. A line snaked down from the aircraft—a rope with a harness attached at the end. I cursed, and the helicopter roar drowned out my curses. All Teddy had to do was attach the painting, and then the chopper would speed away with Larke's masterpiece.

I shouted, "Teddy, we're friends. Please stop."

"If we are friends," he shouted back, "then don't try to stop me."

"But you're stealing."

"A piece of the pie," he shouted. "My piece. For years, everyone else got theirs. Now I want mine."

The helicopter hovered over us. The wind beat against me, shoving me. I nearly toppled over the side of the cabin. But steadied myself at the last moment.

From out on the lake, Mom's voice crackled through a loudspeaker—"Police! Turn back!"—and even that was hard to hear.

The helicopter lowered its rope further and further. The harness swinging over the trees. Coming closer and closer.

"Teddy," I yelled.

Teddy reached up and grabbed the rope, and then glanced my way.

I screamed, "Look out—snake!" And threw the old piece of rope. The wind caught it, and it skittered across the roof.

For a second, it slithered.

That was enough.

Teddy's reaction was instant. He let out a soundless cry, muffled by the roar of the chopper. He dropped the painting with a thunk and staggered backward. But there was no wall behind him and no floor. He stepped into pure air.

"Teddy!"

I lunged at him. But he was too far away.

He fell.

His hand still gripped the helicopter's rope, and it saved him from plummeting to the ground. He swung off the cabin. His weight tugged at the aircraft. The helicopter dipped, then righted itself, lifting Teddy into the air and moving him over the trees.

He howled—not with fear, but with rage.

I picked up the Julia Larke painting, making sure it wasn't damaged.

From the speedboat came Mom's amplified voice: "Park!"

I glanced up just in time to see Teddy on the rope, careening toward me. He lashed out at me, but I ducked, and the effort made him spin on the rope. He struck a tree and crashed through its branches.

He yelled at the helicopter overhead.

But the din was deafening, and now another helicopter appeared over the forest. It sped toward us. Even at a distance, its blue and white colors were unmistakable.

"State police," I yelled into the wind, grinning and giving them a thumbs up.

Arthur X's helicopter pilot must've seen the state police chopper, too. Because the helicopter banked, turned away, and sent Teddy flying over the trees, screaming.

The helicopter rose, lifting Teddy over the rippling waters of the lake. He struggled upward, trying to climb the rope. Did he think he might be saved? That Arthur X would whisk him away? No way. Men like Arthur X didn't care about anyone but themselves.

I was right.

The rope shuddered. Teddy let out a piercing cry that cut through the rotor roar. The rope detached from the helicopter and Teddy fell, and fell, and fell. Then exploded into the water, barreling under the surface.

Arthur X's helicopter accelerated across the lake and over the trees, darting away. The state police chopper followed.

I stared at the water, my heart in my throat. Was Teddy...?

Then he bobbed to the surface, and I let out a breath. Relieved.

From the cabin roof, I watched the Allington PD speedboat glide toward Teddy. With the helicopters gone and the speedboat slowing, the din of engines disappeared. Calm gradually crept back in over the island.

It was over.

30

The crowd at Larke House buzzed with excitement. Miranda pulled the curtain aside, revealing the three paintings. Three stately women at different stages of life, each nude, and each posed in a distinctive way.

"As Julia Larke imagined them," she told the audience, "the three sisters are finally together again."

Applause broke out.

She thanked the museum that had acquired the two sisters for lending them to Larke House. After the exhibition, the two sisters would return to their new home at the museum. "And the third sister will go with them—on loan from Larke House. But once that exhibition is over, she will return to us. A big thank you to Lil Taylor of the Lakeview Inn for her beyond-generous donation of this masterpiece to Larke House."

The audience clapped, and near us, Joy raised a glass and hollered, "Yay, Aunt Lil!"

I nudged Aunt Lil, who was standing next to me, and she smiled. She hadn't even hesitated to donate the painting to

Larke House. Once she learned of its importance, she told me, she didn't doubt where it belonged.

"You're amazing," I said. "You could've sold that painting for half a million dollars, and no one would've judged you. Or you could've charged Miranda a quarter of the price. It still would've been a small fortune."

She shrugged. "My Tarot cards don't lie—this was always the fate of the painting. Besides, it was the right thing to do. Now Larke House will attract even more visitors, which isn't just good for Larke House—it's good for Allington."

I linked arms with her. "You should be mayor."

"Oh, I've got enough to do with the inn, thank you very much."

Mom and Dad passed us. Dad with a glass of wine, Mom with a glass of mineral water in her hand. She was wearing her uniform, but was taking the opportunity to mingle with people, and apparently enjoying it. My dad stood on tiptoe to kiss her.

"Hey," I said. "Not in front of the kids."

Mom smiled and said, "What a happy ending."

"For most of us," I said.

Months had passed since Teddy's arrest, and he'd stand trial soon. But Arthur X's helicopter had escaped capture, and although the authorities had charged the billionaire with conspiring to steal the painting, he was likely only to face a small fine. It felt unfair.

When I shared my feelings aloud, Dad nodded.

"People like Arthur X always get away with murder," he said. "Or at least with attempted theft."

"It's sad," Mom said.

"But true," I added.

Mom and Dad moved off. A long line had formed, with

people shuffling slowly past the three masterpieces. Among them were my siblings Amy and Ray—along with his wife, Roxie—as well as Balthazar from Balthazar Books in his wire-rim glasses and pointy goatee. I overheard a couple talk excitedly about how amazing the art was. Julia Larke was finally getting the respect she deserved.

Aunt Lil and I hung back. Miranda had already treated us to a private viewing of the triptych. As people passed us, I spotted Esther Winch and Knox Kensington talking to each other.

Esther was saying, "Really, if it hadn't been for the early articles I published on Julia Larke, none of this would've happened…"

"Bishop & Company," Knox said, "and—dare I say, myself—deserve much of the credit. If it weren't for us…"

Aunt Lil chuckled. "What do I always tell you, Park? People are predictable. Their behavior is written in the stars."

We headed over to the Larke House entrance and its new gift shop. From inside the store, Scottie called out. "Hey, sis, how about a three sisters t-shirt? Or a mug?"

I laughed. "Maybe later."

"Oh, come on," he said. "Where's your town pride? It's embarrassing that only out-of-towners walk around with Larke House t-shirts. Plus, you're supporting your brother."

"You sure know how to guilt-trip someone into buying stuff."

Scottie beamed. "It's my superpower."

In the end, Aunt Lil and I both bought t-shirts. Sure, his guilt-tripping worked. But I also wanted to support his new business. His and Miranda's.

They'd found the perfect compromise. Miranda needed a gift shop and Scottie wanted to sell Larke merchandise.

This way Scottie got exclusivity while respecting Miranda's rights. And since they shared profits, they were both happy.

In fact, that could be said of all of us in Allington: peace was restored and everyone was happy. Aunt Lil and I headed out of Larke House and into the sunshine.

"Mom's right," I said.

"Oh?" she said.

Linking arms with her, I smiled. "This is a happy ending."

~

THANK YOU for reading this Parker Lee Mystery. Want more? Check out another mystery with Park and her family in:

The Deadly Circle

Want a **free short story**? Sign up for my newsletter to hear when the next book comes out and I'll share the story with you:

https://mpblackbooks.com/newsletter/

If you enjoyed this book, please take a moment to **leave a review online**. It makes it easier for other readers to find the book. Thanks so much!

Turn the page to read an excerpt from *The Deadly Circle...*

31

EXCERPT FROM THE DEADLY CIRCLE

It began with a whisper: "Hey, Park."

Someone tapped me on the shoulder. My brother Scottie, sitting in the pew behind me. I frowned at him and raised a finger to my lips. Typical of Scottie to be talking during the Sunday service.

I turned back around, focusing my attention on my sister Amy.

Amy, pastor at Shepherd's Gate Church, was standing by the lectern. She wore a white robe with a stole hanging over her shoulders. Light from the tall stained-glass windows behind her shone down on her.

"I want to tell you a story," she told us, her congregation, her amplified voice reverberating into the rafters. "It comes to us from the stories of Buddha. It's about Aṅgulimāla, a cruel brigand. A killer."

She told the story of the brigand, and how he took the first steps toward redemption by becoming a monk—and then, helping a woman through a difficult childbirth, he became a man who brought life instead of death to the village.

Before Amy even finished the lesson, I got her point: even the worst of us could find redemption through our actions. A classic Amy sermon. And I was thinking about how it might apply to my own life, when Scottie tapped my shoulder again.

I turned around. "Settle down," I hissed.

"But, Park—"

He motioned at something beyond me. What was he pointing at? Despite my irritation, I turned to look. My curiosity usually trumps my annoyance—even at Scottie, who can be pretty annoying.

He was gesturing at someone, not something. A man sitting a few pews ahead of us, across the aisle. Short, black hair. Oxford shirt, untucked. Jeans. Loafers. No socks. Even seeing only his profile, I recognized him.

I sucked in my breath.

"It's him," Scottie said, "isn't it?"

I nodded. "Ken Tora."

Ken Tora wasn't just famous in Allington. People all over the country—all over the world—knew about Ken Tora. He was one of those Silicon Valley start-up dudes whose name had become synonymous with easy money and fast-lane success. In Allington, of course, he was proudly remembered as "one of ours." Born and raised.

"What's he doing back in Allington?" I wondered out loud.

"I don't know. But we should find out. And I'm definitely pitching at least one business idea to him."

I winced. Scottie wasn't kidding. On top of owning Scottie's Ice Cream Shop and Allington Bike Rentals, my youngest of two older brothers always had half a dozen side hustles and a hundred startup ideas floating around.

"Before you scare him off, let me talk to him first," I said. "Can you imagine if I landed an interview with Ken Tora?"

"Dad would be happy."

"So would *The Gazette*'s readers," I said.

"Shh..." Mom, who sat to my left, nudged me.

To her left sat Joy, my other sister. Next to her was Ray, my oldest brother. Dad was the last one in the pew.

If you lived in Allington, you couldn't escape the Lee family. Mom was the chief of police of our little town. Joy ran Café Larke and Pure Joy Yoga Studio on Peony Lane. Ray owned the Lake Breeze Brewery—or simply "The Breeze" to us locals—right down on the docks near Scottie's Ice Cream Shop. And Dad owned *The Allington Gazette*, where I worked as the only full-time reporter.

As a teen, I'd felt stifled by my family. They were, quite literally, everywhere I turned. So I'd escaped to college and after that to the big city to work at a national newspaper.

But I lost my job and came home, with my tail tucked between my legs.

Only to discover that Allington was pretty neat.

Maybe Ken Tora was discovering the same thing. In fact, he looked engrossed in Amy's story about the brigand-turned-monk. Mesmerized. The only times he took his eyes off my sister, he bent over a notebook and scribbled furiously.

When the service ended and the coffee hour began, Ken shot to his feet and pushed through the crowd toward my sister. On my side of the aisle, it took longer to get out.

I wove my way past the congregants, and by the time I got to Amy and Ken, they were deep in conversation already. I waited. No point interrupting. In fact, I wanted to make a good impression.

Amy said, "I'm happy to meet with you, if you'd like to talk more."

Ken scratched his neck. "I guess that'd be good…"

"Come to my office after coffee hour."

She smiled at him. His own smile was weak. Uncertain. Not the kind of smile I was used to seeing in news articles or on social. Where was the confident Ken Tora I knew from the media?

He turned away from Amy. Here was my chance. Out of the corner of my eye, I spotted a familiar figure swooping in. Scottie. As quickly as I could, I grabbed Ken's arm and spun him away from Scottie.

"Ken," I said, as if we were old friends. "Could we talk? I'm from *The Allington Gazette*, and I'd love to—"

He stiffened, his eyes widening.

"No," he muttered, pulling his arm from my grasp. "Not right now."

Inwardly, I cursed myself. Too direct. Barreling right into the topic.

He ducked past me. Scottie bore down on him. But Ken must have an elevator-pitch radar, because he swerved around my brother, and like a halfback speeding down the football field, streaked down the aisle. Heading straight for the exit.

Ken stopped. A sudden, jarring stop. A man with slicked-back hair and an angular, fox-like face leaned against the doorway, his arms crossed. Smiling at Ken.

As Ken approached—slowly, cautiously—the guy nodded at him and threw an arm around his shoulders. Even at a distance, I could see he gripped Ken firmly, guiding him out of the church.

Before vanishing into the bright Sunday sunshine, Ken cast a glance backward, a frown on his face. A worried frown. I stared at the emptiness he left behind, wondering what could worry Ken Tora.

"Bummer," Scottie said. "Next time, eh, Park?"

"Yeah. Next time."

~

Want more? Grab *The Deadly Circle* at your favorite online bookstore.

MORE BY M.P. BLACK

A Wonderland Books Cozy Mystery Series

A Bookshop to Die For

A Theater to Die For

A Halloween to Die For

A Christmas to Die For

A Yarn Shop to Die For

A Hair Salon to Die For

An Italian-American Cozy Mystery Series

The Soggy Cannoli Murder

Sambuca, Secrets, and Murder

Tastes Like Murder

Meatballs, Mafia, and Murder

Parker Lee Mystery Series

The Art of Murder

The Deadly Circle

Trouble Brewing

A Killer View

Short stories

The Italian Cream Cake Murder (FREE)

ABOUT THE AUTHOR

M.P. Black writes fun cozies with an emphasis on food, books, and travel—and, of course, a good old murder mystery.

Besides writing and publishing his own books, he helps others fulfill their author dreams too through courses and coaching.

M.P. Black has lived in many places, including Brooklyn, Vienna, and San Jose de Costa Rica. Today, he and his family live in Copenhagen, Denmark, where coziness ("hygge") is a national pastime.

Join M.P. Black's free newsletter to download a free story and get updates on books and special deals:

https://mpblackbooks.com/newsletter/